Happy reading

Cover design and typesetting: Macha Yao

Leapwise Publishing
ISBN: 978-1-0685447-0-5

Tempest's Secret

Brave kids never give up

Ariane Chapelle

Illustrated by Macha Yao

To Talitha and Tristan,
my beloved Tempest and Wallace in real life.

Chapter 1
The plea

'Wallace, go and ask Mum for a pet,' I tell my little brother.

It would be so cool to have a pet. Wallace and I would have a little friend to play with—so cute and so much fun. Mum and Dad are always working or travelling for work, so they don't play with us much. We're bored at home, but they always say no to a pet. Maybe this time Mum will say yes if Wallace asks her.

Wallace is eight, three years younger than me. He's annoying sometimes, but he does everything I ask and follows me everywhere, jumping around and playing games. Wallace only sees the bright side of life and the good in people. He's the opposite of me; I trust animals more than humans; animals are truthful. **I would CRY for joy** if I had a pet. Especially a cat. I know everything about cats: how they grow, what they eat, what they like and dislike. I know how to behave around them and how to respect their character and independence so that they trust you and come to you. Cats are free and proud, like me.

'Tempest, not again!' my brother grumbles.

Yep, my name is Tempest: like a raging storm, when the wind blows, the sky turns dark before lightning strikes, and the thunder rages like an angry monster. Mum and Dad chose my name before they could know if I would be a quiet girl with long, plaited blond hair and a soft voice. I would have been ridiculous with a name like Tempest and a look like Alice in Wonderland. It turns out they were right: I don't look like Alice in Wonderland. I have thick, brown hair that tangles like crazy when I run. And I run everywhere I go because walking is so slow; it's boring. I'm skinny, and I wear leggings and tiny tee shirts. I look like a broomstick upside down.

'Why me?' insists Wallace.

My brother looks doubtful. He thinks I'm trying to get him into trouble, but I'm not. At least not this time.

'Because she always says yes to you. You're her favourite.'

'I'm not,' replies Wallace with a frowny face.

He hates it when I call him the favourite, but Wallace IS Mum's favourite, the younger one, the only boy. We have a big sister too, but she lives in New York for her studies. Mum says yes to things for Wallace even though she says no to me. That's because he pretends to cry to avoid getting into trouble. It works every time with Mum. If someone can convince Mum to have a pet, it's Wallace.

'Yes, you are. Go and ask for a cat. *Please.* Wouldn't you be happy to have a little cat to play with, Wallace?' I ask, sure of what he's going to say.

'Yes! Yes!'

'Then go. I will be right behind you. I'll hide,' I add to encourage him.

Wallace walks to the living room. Mum's sitting at the table, working on her computer, even though it's Sunday. Mum's always working on her computer like it's her favourite thing in the world.

'Muuuum?' Wallace always calls Mum by dragging on the 'uuuu.'

'What now?!' Mum snaps, 'Do you realise that you call me every two minutes, Wallace?'

I listen from around the corner. Mum sounds annoyed; now is not a good time.

'Hum... nothing,' says my brother, already racing back to his room as fast as he can on his little legs.

Mum's in a bad mood, and she's scary when she's mad. I should have checked before sending Wallace. Never mind, we'll try some other time. I run upstairs and join my brother in his room: he's sitting on his bed, arms crossed, lips tight. I can see a tear at the corner of his eye.

'I told you I wasn't her favourite,' he says, 'it's all ruined now, and it's all your fault!'

'OK. Now was not the time, but we'll try again,' I reply, ignoring his attack. 'Brave kids never give up.'

'We'll never have a cat.' Wallace is sulking, but he's easy to distract. And I'm hungry.

'How about baking a cake?' I try.

'Yes, yes!' My brother bounces back like a puppy excited by a new game. I may not have a pet, but I have Wallace who is full of energy and joy of life. He's always up for cake, chocolate, or candies.

I lead us to the kitchen, Wallace hopping behind me. He hops every time he can, like a mini kangaroo. Dad was born in Australia, so maybe Wallace inherited a kangaroo gene.

'What are you guys doing?' Mum has heard us. She calls from the living room, turning her head to check on us, but she doesn't leave her chair.

'Nothing,' I say.

'Baking,' says Wallace at the same time: he's not very good at lying.

‘OK, be good,’ Mum replies. She clearly did not listen. When Mum’s working, a marching band could parade through the living room, and she wouldn't even notice. Dad’s the same. I don’t know what’s so interesting on adults’ computers to keep them so occupied. Maybe I’ll find out when I grow up. I think it’s crazy: a pet is so much more exciting than a computer!

I close the kitchen door behind Wallace and me, so Mum can’t hear us anymore anyway.

‘OK, let’s bake a yummy cake with chocolate and candies. What do you think?’ I ask my little brother, sure of the answer. ‘But you have to do what I say.’

‘Yes, yes!’ Wallace hops around the kitchen like a wallaby on a sugar rush, though we haven’t eaten anything yet. He pulls out the baking tins and bowls as I ask. Wallace is always happy to help, and he loves cooking. I don’t: I like sweets and finger food. I could live only on chocolate and cereal bars, but Mum makes us eat carrot sticks at every lunch and doesn’t allow chocolate before mealtime.

It’s nearly lunchtime, but she can’t see me. So, I stand on my tippy toes to grab a chocolate pack from the shelf. I can feel my mouth watering at the idea of eating the delicious creamy squares. But just as I break a big piece off the bar, I hear footsteps behind the door. Mum's coming: trouble ahead!

'Wallace, catch!'

I throw the chocolate into Wallace's hands just before Mum opens the door. Wallace is standing in the middle of the kitchen, holding the piece of chocolate with both hands, mouth open, eyes wide, stiff as a statue. Better that he gets into trouble rather than me. He's her soft spot anyway.

'Wallace!' shouts Mum, 'What's that?'

My brother stands still, looks at me, looks at Mum. His mouth is still open, but no sound is coming out. Tears are mounting in his eyes. I start feeling a bit guilty, but he gets me into trouble sometimes, too.

'But we want a caaaaat!' he finally cries.

Mum gasps, then laughs. She puts away the chocolate and sits us around the kitchen table.

'Listen, you two,' she starts. I get ready for another lecture. Mum loves lecturing us. She holds our hands, looks us straight in the eyes, and we'd better listen.

'We have been through this before. I know you want a pet, but Daddy and I disagree. A pet needs care and presence. You are at school all day, and Daddy and I travel a lot for work. Who will take care of this poor pet, huh? Not your grandmother: she can barely look after you two when we're away! Plus, London is a big city, with many cars and other dangers for animals. If you get emotionally attached to a pet and something happens to him, you would be very sad. Daddy and I don't want that.'

'OK...' I say, looking down. I already knew what Mum was going to say. She always says the same thing, but she's wrong. I would be great at taking care of a pet. I know loads about animals, and I understand them. I can tell the species and age of a cat, a dog, or a hamster just by looking at them. I even know what they mean to say by the noise they make. But Mum will never agree, and there's no point arguing with her. It's unfair. She doesn't understand how happy I would be if I had a pet to love.

'Noooooow, can I have some chocolate?' asks Wallace, who never misses an opportunity to turn a problem into a chance to eat. I wish I could see the world as playfully as he does.

'No sugar before mealtime, you know that,' lectures Mum again. 'Worse, you tried to eat some without my permission. What are the two most important rules in the family?'

'Never lie, and always speak with respect,'

Wallace and I answer at the same time. We know. Mum repeats the rules at every chance she gets. Telling the truth is how we build trust in a family, she says, and there is nothing more important than trusting each other. Mum gets furious when we mess up with the rules. And no one wants to be around when Mum is furious.

I run away to my room, hiding my tears. I want to be alone with my soft toys: my sweet Lana from The Lion King, who sleeps in my arms every night; Pingy the giant penguin that I use as a pillow; Tucker, my fury spaniel who looks like Copper in the Fox and the Hound; and Old Bunny, my pink fluffy rabbit from when I was a baby. For a long time, I could pretend they were real. It's harder now: I'm not a little girl anymore. I need a real pet and real adventures. I don't know that my life is about to change forever.

Chapter 2
Climbing trees

'Kiiiiiids, lunch is ready!' Mum drags out the vowels just like Wallace, though she hates it when he does it to her. People don't like seeing their own flaws back in others, I think. We hurry to the kitchen. Mum doesn't want us to be late. Mum does everything fast, and she doesn't like to wait.

Like everything else, Mum prepared our lunch quickly: breaded chicken in the oven, quick-cooking spaghetti with bottled tomato sauce, and carrot sticks. Next to our plates, she put two squares of milk chocolate as dessert, the same I tried to grab earlier. Wallace and I eat in silence while Mum goes back to the living room table that she uses as her desk.

'Tempest, can we go to the park, pleeeaaase!' asks Wallace out of the blue.

'Of course, that's a good idea! Let's finish our lunch, and we'll go.'

The park next to our house is my happy place. It's so lucky that we live close to a park in London; we can just walk out on the street, turn right, walk for a minute, and there we are. It's so close that Mum lets us go on our own, which is great. Otherwise, I think I would die of boredom at home.

I slide the carrot sticks into my leggings' pocket. Tip and Tap will be happy later. Tip and Tap are my squirrel friends from the park that I tamed. Playing with animals is my favourite thing in the world: they're friendly and affectionate—not like a lot of people. I'm not very good at making human friends. I don't fit in. Why should I follow the latest fashion trends, know the life of celebrities, or look like everyone else? People are mean when you're not like them, but that's ok: I find other ways to make friends and be happy.

'Mum, we've finished lunch. Can we go to the park now, please?' I ask as soon as I have swallowed my last bit of chicken.

'Of course, guys. Have fun. Tempest, not too high in the trees, please,' replies Mum, still sitting in front of her computer.

I climb trees faster than anyone. I know I'm tiny for my age, and I hate it when people call me Shorty. Yet when I'm on top of a tree, I'm taller than everybody. I share tree branches with the birds. Mum says I'm like a robin, but that's because it's the only type of bird she knows. They're easy to spot with their orange patch on their chests. Mum doesn't know much about animals. I'm more like a magpie: clever, curious, and independent. I know all the birds in the park and their different characters. I wish I could fly like them and feel free.

The trees in our park are my friends, too; I give them names. The biggest one is an elm: his branches start low and spread widely across the middle of the grass, protecting us from the rain or the sun when we play and hide. I called him Elmo, obviously, like in Sesame Street. Elmo's trunk is so big that I can't even cover half its circumference when I spread my arms around it. Given its size, Elmo is at least a hundred years old. He's as tall as a four-storey building. I haven't climbed him near its top yet, but I wanted to try before my next birthday, before I'm 12. I got this.

The sky is bright blue, without a cloud to see. It's

one of those toasty days of September in London, before the weather turns grey and rainy for six months. Then, Mum will force me to wear a jumper and a jacket: when she gets cold, I am the one who must wrap up.

Wallace kicks the football with his friends, and I play with Tip, my favourite squirrel, sitting on the grass. Tip likes the carrot sticks I pull out of my leggings for him. I sing 'A Smile and a Song' like Snow White to the birds and squirrels in the Disney movie. Tip likes it when I sing to him. I LOVE Disney songs; I know all of them by heart. I'm as pale as Snow White, but my hair is way wilder, and I definitely don't dream of Prince Charming. Eek! The other kids at my school are trying to have boyfriends and girlfriends. But not for me, thank you!

As I finish my song, I hear a faint '*meeooowww*' coming from above. I look up, but the sun shines right into my eyes, and I can't see anything. Another 'MEOW!' repeats louder. Wallace has heard the noise now, too. He abandons his football and runs to me. We walk around the park slowly, trying to locate the sound. It's coming from Elmo!

'MEOW! MEEOOOWWWW!' It's a kitten in distress!

I must climb and rescue him. Wallace wants to follow me.

Putting one foot on a branch and one hand on a branch, I start my way up. I know I can do this, even on a massive tree like Elmo. It's easy, I'm progressing fast.

I can hear the noise, but I can't find any cat; there are so many branches, and the foliage is so thick. I keep moving up, looking everywhere I can.

The branches are getting thinner as I climb higher. I must be careful. One foot at a time, one branch at a time…

I'm so high now that I can see the whole park and up until our street, beyond the gates: the red and white brick houses, the rooftops, the terraces. I swallow and take a deep breath. I'm not scared, of course I'm not... I think I'm not.

Down below, people look small. I know everyone in our park: Wallace's friends who play football, my neighbour friend and her mum, who buys us ice cream, the old granny with purple hair who always reads the same book…but who's that?

There is a stranger in our park. From high up, I can see him pushing the gate onto the street. His face is hidden by a soft grey hat with no real shape, like a melting cake. There's curly grey hair coming out of his hat, like frizzy decorations around the cake. He must be an old man: he walks slowly, leaning forward, holding his hands behind his back. He wears brown baggy pants and soft shoes, like slippers. He walks like he's sliding on the pavement, as if he's ice-skating.

Just when he's about to turn the street corner and disappear, the man stops. He looks up, right at the top of the tree. He's looking at me! Even from that height, I can see his steely blue eyes, a piercing gaze that gives me shivers.

CRAAAACKKKK !!! AAAHHHHHH !!!

Wallace! I was so busy observing the steely blue-eyed stranger that I forgot about my little brother following me up the tree. He needs help. He must have stepped on a weaker branch that cracked under his weight. Wallace is still small, but he's muscly and heavy, like a dumbbell. He falls through the twigs and is suddenly stopped by a big branch:

OUCH!!!

MMMMEEEEEOWWWW!!!

Wallace has found the cat.

More precisely, Wallace has fallen on the cat.

He has scratches on his face and twigs in his hair, but he's not injured. Most of all, Wallace is super proud to have found the cat all by himself.

It's a black kitten; only the tip of his right paw is white, and the top of his chest, like a mini bib for a baby cat. 'Come here, my sweetie', I whisper to the kitten, reaching towards him. I sit on a branch and take him into my arms. He's too dizzy to protest. Wallace has fallen on the side of him, and he's not hurt, just a bit drowsy with the fright and the shock. I hold the kitten in my arms like a tiny baby. I pet him on the head and under the chin. I know kittens like that. He starts purring and I can tell he's feeling better already. He must be six or seven weeks old, with beautiful greeny-blue-y eyes. The blue eyes all kittens have at birth are turning green for him. My heart is melting with love for my new best friend already.

'It looks like he has a pompom on his leg,' says Wallace, pointing at the kitten's white paw in the black fur.

'That's an idea! Let's call him "Pompon", then!' I say. 'Good job Wallace! Now, let's get down and take care of Pompon.'

Wallace climbs down first, his little legs dangling in the air before reaching the next branch down, but he manages. I follow him carefully, holding the branches with one arm and Pompon safe with the other. I'm responsible for another life now. I must be careful.

We jump on the ground from the last tree branch. My brother has a big smile on his face. My heart is pounding with joy and excitement. We are so proud to have saved an animal. Pompon has no collar, no tattoo, and no sign of any owner. He could be our cat. Mum and Dad won't be happy, but I love Pompon so much already. Brave kids never give up. We must find a way.

Chapter 3
The secret pet

'Wallace, go and check if Mum's home, please!'

We're walking back from the park. Pompon is in my arms, hidden under my hand. No one should know we have a pet yet, especially Mum and Dad. Otherwise, they might force us to give it up to a vet or an animal refuge, and I would DIE of sadness from losing him. That's not an option. Pompon will be our secret pet until it's safe to tell our parents. I have a plan, sort of.

'Here, catch!' I throw the house keys to my brother, who grabs them like a real cricket player and runs to the house. A few seconds later, Wallace opens the front door and tiptoes around the hallway.

'Hellooooo! Anyone hooooome?' Only the ticking clock in the living room answers his calls. There's a note from Mum on the buffet in the hallway:

'Gone to pick up Manie at the airport. Back in about two hours. Be good. Love, Mum.'

Manie's our grandmother, mum's mum. She's 70 years old, but she tells everyone she's 62. 'I'm stuck at 62,' she says. We don't know how long she'll be stuck for. Sometimes people look at her oddly: it could be because she looks a bit older than she pretends or because she always wears crazy clothes. Besides funny fashion, Manie loves travels and photos. Her living room is full of photo souvenirs from around the world: the pyramids of Egypt, the Taj Mahal in India, Christ the Redeemer in Brazil... She said that next year, she will take us with her on one of her trips—I'm so excited!

Today, she's coming back from a photo safari in Tanzania. Every time she comes back from a trip, Mum picks her up from the airport and Manie has tea or dinner with us to tell us firsthand her most gripping memories and adventures. Manie always has fun stories to tell. I wonder what it will be this time.

It's lucky Mum's out for now, but she could be

back any time, so we don't have a minute to waste.

'OK, Wallace, let's follow the plan,' I say to my little brother, trying to sound calm and organised. 'Can you help?'

'Yes, yes! I can, I can!' Wallace agrees twice and hops around on one leg—the two unmistakable signs that he's happy and excited.

'Great. First, let's find something to eat and drink for Pompon,' I say, going to the kitchen. Pompon becomes wriggly in my arms. He wants to discover his new place, but I can't let him wander in the living room. Mum would find cat hair on the cushions or marks on the floor and carpets; we'd be caught out in no time.

'Close the kitchen door really well so Pompon can't escape. Otherwise, we'd get into real trouble, understand?' I warn my brother, 'I don't want to lose him over a silly mistake.'

'OK,' he says, pushing the kitchen door closed with both hands. 'And now, let's give some milk to Pompon!'

'No, not milk. It will hurt his tummy. We'll give him water instead. Kittens need their mother's milk when they're little babies. After, they should drink only water.' I explain, happy to be able to finally apply everything I learnt about kittens.

I let Pompon jump off my arms onto the kitchen floor. I pour fresh water in a bowl. Pompon laps it quickly, with the funniest creaking noise—he's so cute. His tiny body needs solid food, too. I grab a slice of cooked chicken in the fridge and cut it into small pieces on a plate next to the bowl. I make sure that food and water don't mix. Cats don't like that.

Wallace and I sit on the floor, watching our new kitten drink and eat with appetite. It feels like a dream: we have a pet. It seems too good to be true.

Once he's finished, I clean up and put everything back in the fridge precisely as it was. Dad would notice immediately if something had been moved. Dad notices the strangest things. He will be back tonight from his business trip to Tokyo, in Japan. It is a super long trip on the plane, and I will be asleep when he comes home. I will see him after school tomorrow. Dad is super fun. I wonder which souvenir he will bring back for us this time: he always brings back little toys from his trips for Wallace and me.

'No, Wallace, don't give him that!' I shout, as

I see my brother about to give a chocolate chip cookie to Pompon. I got distracted for just a second, enough for Wallace to take a new initiative.

'Why not? It's yummy,' he asks, puzzled. Pompon turns to me, too—now both are looking at me with a dark look and a wrinkled nose. It's hard not to laugh!

'Chocolate is toxic for cats: Pompon could be very sick. Don't let him have any. Pompon needs his own food, but you can eat the cookie if you want,' I smile.

Pompon loses interest in the cookie and starts wandering around the kitchen, sniffing the table and chairs, exploring every corner. We watch him in silence, Wallace nibbling on his cookie. Pompon walks under the kitchen table, stops, squats, and…

'Loooooook! He's doing a wee-wee on the flooooor!' laughs my brother. **'Yuuuuucckkk! It stinks!'** he winces. The smelly pee brings me back to reality. Mum will be home any minute, and I need a litter box, kitten food, and a hiding place for Pompon. Having a secret pet is complicated. I can't panic, it'll be alright. Deep breath.

'Hold him while I clean, please,' I say to my brother, putting Pompon in his arms. 'Keep him snug, like a little baby.'

'Yes, yes,' says Wallace, sticking his tongue out. Wallace sticks out his tongue every time he concentrates on doing something new.

'Let's hide Pompon in my room,' I say.

My brother nods in silence: Pompon has fallen asleep in his arms. Kittens sleep a lot, and Pompon has had a big day. We go upstairs and lay our friend on a comfy blanket on my bed. With his eyes closed and fluffy fur, Pompon looks just like another one of my soft toys. Only his little chest going up and down shows that he's alive.

'I'll run out quickly to get cat litter and kitten food. I'll be back as fast as I can.' I say to my brother while putting all the money from my piggy bank in my legging's pocket. 'Don't go anywhere: stay in my room with Pompon. Keep the door closed and watch him, please. And don't let him poo on my soft toys either!'

'Ahahaha, OK,' giggles Wallace.

'I'm serious, Wallace. Can I count on you?' I look straight at my brother. He can't mess up.

'Yes, yes! Promised, promised!'

I shut my bedroom door tight and start racing down the stairs, sprinting through the house onto the street. There's a pet shop only two streets away. I pass it every day on my way to school, dreaming of having a reason to go in there. Now I do.

'Good afternoon!' I shout, a bit short of breath and louder than I wanted to the lady behind the counter.

'Good afternoon, young lady… where's your Mum?' she asks, looking at me suspiciously. She's tall, skinny, and wears big eyeglasses. With her beige cardigan and her grey hair tied in a bun, she looks more like a librarian than a pet shopkeeper. With my tangled hair and dirty tee shirt, I look more like a homeless kid than a pet owner. Appearances are deceptive.

'She's waiting in the car,' I lie. 'We couldn't find a parking place, so she asked me to come in. We're kind of in a hurry.' I grin, my fingers crossed behind my back, hoping she'll believe my story. 'I need some kitten dry food and a small litter bag, please. For £18.50,' I say as politely as possible, putting all my money on the counter. It's all I have. I hope it's enough. I have no idea how much these things cost. I read all about animals, except for that!

'£18.50? That's very precise, but it's enough,' says the shopkeeper-librarian, as if she could hear my thoughts.

'Here we go young lady,' she says, handing me the bag.

'Thank you very much! Goodbye!' I say, already at the door.

I sprint back home like a cheetah in a rush. Everything's still quiet. Wallace has fallen asleep on my bed next to Pompon. I tiptoe into the bedroom, looking at them both. I don't want to wake up Pompon; he needs a rest.

'Wallace, wake up!' I whisper to my brother, gently shaking his shoulder. 'I need your plastic toy box for Pompon's litter.'

'Noooo, it will smell like horrible peeeee!' he grumbles, half asleep.

'We'll wash it out after. Go!' I order. 'I'll get some other bowls from the kitchen for Pompon's food and water, and we meet back in my room in two minutes.'

I hear the front door slam as I grab the plastic bowls from the kitchen cupboard. I freeze.

‘Helloooo! We’re baaaack!’ calls Mum, walking to the kitchen.

‘Oh, hello, Tempest!

... **What are you doing with these bowls?’**

Chapter 4
Manie

I freeze, standing in the middle of the kitchen, the bowls in my hand. I must think fast, but finding excuses is not my greatest strength.

'... I need to sort out colour beads in my room! For school tomorrow. It's mufti day. I need to make necklaces for charity. For my friends, I mean. Is it ok if I use the bowls for the night?' I'm speaking way too fast and too loud. I can sense a cold sweat running down my spine, and I'm blushing.

Mum looks at me, puzzled: 'You? Sorting out your room?'

My room's always a mess, with clothes on the floor, books and toys mixed up. I hate tidying up; I don't see the point. And why should I make my bed in the morning if it's just to undo it every night anyway? Mum can't be bothered tidying up either most of the time, though she doesn't like seeing the mess around the house. Sometimes, she yells really loud, and I put everything back in place. Until the next time.

'Sure, if you want,' Mum says, still puzzled.

'Thanks, I'll be quick!'

I run out of the kitchen before she asks me any more questions. My hands are shaking. I hate lying to Mum. It's against the rules, and I'm a little ashamed, too, but I have no choice.

I'm so deep in my thoughts that I don't see Manie's suitcase in the middle of the hallway. I run right into it, stumble, and fall flat on my face. The bowls slide out of my hands and go rolling under the buffet.

Lying on the floor, all I see are two slim legs wrapped in white lace, above tanned feet slipped into high-heeled shoes. Manie's standing above me, dressed in her favourite lace trousers, surmounted by a puffy golden jacket. Who could guess she's just come off a plane?

'Whaaaaa Tempest! Where are you going so fast?' Manie says 'whaaaaa' every time she's happy, surprised or scared. 'Come here, give me a hug!' She helps me get up and squishes me with all her might. I feel her golden bangles pressing against my ribs, and her patchouli perfume makes me sneeze.

'**Aaachhhi!** Hi Manie! I'm so happy to see you! But give me a minute, please. I need to go to my room real quick,' I say, picking up the bowls from under the furniture. And, without giving Manie a chance to respond, I run upstairs. Wallace has brought in his toy box, and he's waiting for me, sitting on the floor between the skirt of my school uniform and one shoe.

‘Thank you for the box! Now, please go to the living room to distract Mum and Manie while I finish setting up the room for Pompon.’

‘But what would I tell them? Can you come with me?’ Wallace is nervous, and I am too. We don’t want to lie to Mum, but we don’t want to lose our cat either.

‘You don’t have to say much; just let them talk. Grown-ups love talking about themselves. Ask them questions, anything: ask Manie about her trip, Mum about her work…That’ll keep them busy. You can do it; now go!’

Wallace smiles, puffs out his chest and hops downstairs. He likes being on a mission. Meanwhile, I roll up my clothes, chuck them into the wardrobe and slide my shoes under my bed. I pour the white, sandy cat litter into Wallace’s toy box; it will be Pompon’s toilet. I hope my baby cat knows how to use litter; that his Mummy or someone showed him. I’ll soon find out. I place the box against the wall under my desk, hidden away in case someone comes in, but easy for Pompon to access. I put the bowl of water next to my bed on the side of the wall so people can’t see it either. I just need to pour the dry food into the bowl, and I'm done; it looks like big CocoPops cereal.

'These are NOT colour beads!' A voice behind me makes me jump up and I bang my head under the desk.

'Ouch! Shhhttt, Manie! Close the door, please!' I beg my grandmother who is standing in the door frame, hands on her hips, observing me.

'What's going on in here?' she says, closing the door behind her. I thank her secretly for doing what I ask. Manie's wild, but she can play fair. I'm used to doing everything on my own, but now, I think I might need allies. *Meeeowww:* my baby cat finally wakes up from all the noise. Manie looks towards the bed, eyes wide.

'Whaaaaa! Look at what we have here! Tempest, how did you ever convince your parents to have a pet?'

'I didn't. **It's a secret.** His name is Pompon. Wallace and I found him today. He was stuck in a high tree in the park, and we saved him. Mum and Dad don't know about him yet. Don't say anything, please, Manie. I need more time.'

'Well, well, well! That's a story! And how do

you think you'll get out of this, my darling? Do you expect to convince your Mum to keep a cat in the house after hiding it from her? You know that she doesn't want to hear about any pet! Not even a goldfish! And your dad's the same.' Manie's shaking her head. I'm worried now. My plan doesn't seem so strong after all.

'But if I can prove to Mum and Dad that I can take good care of a pet without causing trouble, even for a few days, they will let me keep him, won't they?' I argue, my voice cracking a little.

'Mmmm, maybe. Not sure, my little chick,' Manie responds, looking at me with pity. That look scares me even more, but I can't give up so soon.

'Well, anyway, Manie. For now, Pompon needs to be a secret between us,' I say, standing back up in front of her. 'Like the day you lost me,' I add, looking straight into her pale green eyes.

When I was six years old, Manie lost me in the crowd at a carnival parade on the seaside. She had stopped to chat with friends and did not see me continuing to follow the parade along the streets, fascinated by the dancers with their green and yellow giants' heads of paper-mâché, moving to the rhythm of the drums. But once the parade was over, I was lost. I was far from Manie's house; I couldn't see her anywhere, and I did not recognise the streets.

I knew that lost kids needed to find a grown-up they could trust and ask for help. All I knew about my address was the name of Manie's house and that it was near the beach. So, I went into a bakery shop and asked the lady behind the counter to call the police to drive me back home. She looked at me with wide eyes, gave me a pain au chocolat and grabbed her phone. Half an hour later, I was dropped in a police van at the 'The Blue Pebbles' in Folkestone.

When I arrived, Manie was sitting next to the phone, staring at the window, twisting her hair around her fingers. Manie only twists her hair when she's really anxious. She had searched for me everywhere frantically, running and yelling my name. A policeman saw her distress, calmed her down and asked her to go back home and wait for me. When I rang the bell, she jumped up like a frog out of boiling water. She opened the door wide and hugged me for a long time. Her eyes were a bit wet when she said, 'Thank you, Officer' to the policeman who brought me back. When he left, Manie held me by the shoulders and asked me to never tell that story to Mum and Dad: 'It will be our secret,' she said. Now we have two.

Manie sees that story in my eyes when I stare at her.

'I see. It's a fair deal,' she replies, looking back at me.

'Good. Now, let's go back to the living room. You go first. I'll be there in a minute.'

I use this short time alone to give Pompon a big cuddle. I whisper in his ear to be quiet and not to worry, that I'll be back soon. I show him his bowls of water and food, and the litter box. I make some paper balls for him to play with. He's looking at me with his cute, green baby eyes. I don't know how much he understands, but he seems to. I give him a last scratch on the head, a last kiss. I close the door tight and go join the others downstairs. I miss my baby cat already.

Everyone's sitting in the living room. Mum has prepared a bowl of chips and glasses of Coca-Cola for Wallace and me. That's a sign it's party time because we're never allowed sugary drinks unless it's a special occasion.

'Mum, are these new shoes?' Mum asks Manie.

'Yep! Snakeskin!' she says, lifting her leg up in the air for everyone to see. 'It was the snake or me. I had stepped out of the jeep for a minute to take better pictures of a family of lions lying in the distance when a cobra slid over to me—its head was lifted, hissing, ready to bite. John, my ranger, saw it just in time: he caught the snake by the tail, then grabbed its head and cut it off with his knife. We had snake for dinner that night, and I had some new shoes made.'

'Snake for dinner! Yuck!' says Wallace.

'It's not bad. Tastes like a mix between chicken and fish.'

'Well, I don't have snake for dinner, but I have pepperoni pizza,' announces Mum, with a wink to Wallace.

'Yes, yes! Pepperoni pizza, pepperoni pizza!' Wallace hops around the living room. Wallace loves pizza like Garfield loves lasagna. The thought of Garfield reminds me of my own cat, alone in my room. I take a deep breath, trying to calm my heart clenching in my chest.

'Mum, can I help you with dinner?' I ask to distract myself.

‘Yes, thank you, Tempest. Please take the pizzas out of the fridge but wait for me to turn the oven on. I forgot my glasses upstairs, I’ll be back. I think I might have left them in your room earlier.’

Before I can say a word, Mum’s already at the staircase. I watch her go in disbelief. This can’t be happening. Manie looks at me. Wallace stops jumping. We are all waiting in silence for the storm to break.

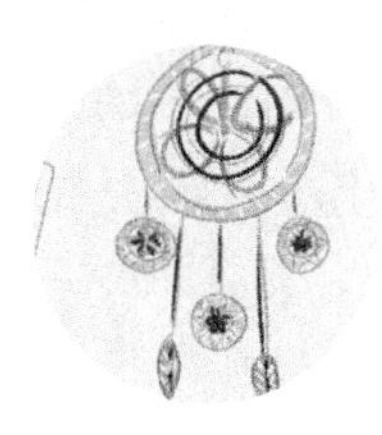

Chapter 5
Night games

'Found them,' says Mum, walking down the stairs, waving her glasses around.

I'm bracing for more, but she doesn't seem upset. Where did she find her reading glasses? Mum loses them ten times a day. For her birthday, I'll get her a glasses chain.

'Mum, everything OK?' I ask with a tiny voice.

'Yes. Why?'

'Nothing.' *Did Mum go to my room? Did she see Pompon? Why isn't she upset?* I am dying to know, but I don't dare to ask any more questions. I look at Manie. She glances back at me and shrugs her shoulders as if to say: 'I don't know either.' I can't wait to go check upstairs. Dinner lasts for what feels like an eternity, though Wallace devours his pizza without much concern. Wallace is never much concerned about anything anyway.

'Tempest, may I have your last slice of pizza if you don't eat it?' he asks, still chewing his last mouthful.

'Sure, here you go.'

I have stomach cramps, and my chest is tight. I just want this to be over. I wriggle in my chair. Manie notices my trouble, gives me a wink and stands up.

'Darling, thank you for having me and for the pizza. It was wonderful,' she says to Mum, brushing imaginary crumbs off her lace trousers, 'but it's time for me to go home now and unpack.' That's a lie. Manie doesn't like pizza; she only pretended to eat. She slid her slices onto Wallace's plate when Mum wasn't looking. Manie eats like a mouse: very little, and mostly cheese and toasts. She never unpacks her suitcase either; she just plunks it in a corner of her bedroom and pulls out clothes as she needs to wear them or wash them. When the suitcase is empty, she finally puts it away or repacks it for another trip. I bet Manie's bedroom is even messier than mine.

'Are you sure?' asks Mum, more out of politeness than a real desire to see her stay. Mum and Manie get on well as long as they don't see each other much. After two hours, it gets tense. After two days, the tension between them flares up like fireworks.

'Let me drive you home,' Mum continues, confirming that her question did not really require an answer.

'That's OK, my darling. Stay with the children. I gave you enough work today already. It's a short ride, so I'll call an Uber. Do you know Uber? It's incredibly convenient when I don't have my car! I even have the app—my friend Yvonne showed me how to use it: look! He will be here in a minute.' Manie's funny—she can barely use a smartphone, but she's keen to try and live with her time.

'Goodbye, my little chick; goodbye, my big boy. I'll see you again soon,' Manie turns to us and hugs us tight. She smiles at me and give me with another big wink. She's so obvious; she'll get us caught! I know she means well, but I can't wait for her to go now.

'Goodbye Manie! See you soon!' I say, without giving Manie the chance to hang around too much longer. 'Mum, let me help you with the plates,' I'm standing up already, holding my plate.

'Wallace will help me,' I add, staring at my brother so he gets up without a protest. I clear everything out as fast as I can and pull Wallace aside in the kitchen.

'I'll pretend to feel sick to go to bed. You stay with Mum and make sure she doesn't come to my room, OK?' I whisper in his ear. He nods and gives me a thumb-up. My heart fills with gratitude for my helpful little brother.

'What are you both up to?' says Mum, coming in, 'You look like conspirators.'

'What's constipators?' asks Wallace.

'Conspirators,' I correct him.

'They're people who prepare some evil plan. We are not.' I explain, looking at Mum. 'But my tummy hurts, Mummy, and I'm tired. That's what I was saying to Wallace. I'll go to bed now, so I'll be fine for school tomorrow!' I grin. I sound so fake. I bite my lips, afraid that Mum will get suspicious. But she doesn't, or at least pretends not to. *Maybe she understood everything and is waiting to see how far I go? Maybe it's a trap?* My hands are shaking. I slide them in my legging pockets, so Mum doesn't see.

'As you wish, sweetie,' she says, kissing me on

the forehead. 'Have a good sleep. I hope you'll feel better in the morning.'

'Byyyyyye Tempest!' says Wallace, waving both hands in the air as if I was leaving for a cruise trip around the world.

'Muuuuuuuum, can I have ice cream for dessert, pleeeaaaase?' Wallace is always trying to get more food, like a hungry squirrel. He knows how to keep Mum occupied by asking one thing after another until she sends him to his room, too, to be in peace. He understands how to behave with adults to get what he wants. I wish I had his skill.

I open my bedroom door very slowly, very carefully, in case Pompon tries to escape. But I feared for nothing: my baby cat isn't behind the door. He's not on my bed either, among my toys, under my bed, behind the curtains or even under the carpet. I look for him, faster and faster, tears mounting in my eyes. I can't breathe; it's like a giant hand is squeezing my throat. *Mum has found Pompon, she's taken him away; she put him out somewhere, and I will never see him again. It's a disaster.*

I crawl on hands and knees, whispering: 'Pompon, Pompon, my baby, where are you?' No answer. I collapse on the floor, desperate. But with my ear on the carpet, I hear a faint scratching noise: **shrrrkkk, shhhrrkkk**. It's coming from behind my bed. A soft '*meeooowww*' brings me back to life. Pompon!

I jump up like a jack-in-the-box, pulling out the pillows and soft toys and sending them flying to the other end of my bed. My baby cat is stuck between the bed and the wall: kittens find the most improbable places to get themselves into! *Meeeooowww*, a little furry head is popping out of the bed frame, looking at me: 'Help me get out of here!' his baby eyes say.

I slide my hands under him and pull gently. He wriggles out of my arms and pounces to his bowl of water, lapping with a noisy 'slurp, slurp, slurp.' Thirsty Pompon! I lie on the floor next to him, recovering from my emotions, tears of relief rolling down my cheeks. The giant hand has let go of my throat; I feel as if I were wrapped up in a warm, soft blanket instead.

I crawl onto my bed. Pompon has stopped drinking and jumps up next to me. He curls up against my chest. I'm still wearing my day clothes, covered in grass stains, my hair as tangled as ever.

I haven't brushed my hair, and I haven't brushed my teeth; I am all dirty, but it doesn't matter. I have a real kitten to sleep with me, and that's the most wonderful feeling in the world. We fall asleep just like that after this incredible day.

In my dreams, I climb a mountain simply with my hands and feet—no rope, no hooks. As I am about to reach the summit, a giant cat is facing me, blocking the way, pressing my nose with his white paw. He presses and presses. I can't climb up anymore.

I wake up. Pompon's paw is pressing on my nose. He wants to play. He walks over my face and sits on my hair spread on the pillow: **Meeeoooowww** he says, tilting his head.

'Good morning to you, too,' I murmur, half asleep. The purple glow of my alarm clock shows 5.05 am. 'It's early, you know. Aren't you sleepy? I am. Let's go back to sleep,' I say, more hopeful than convinced. I wrap myself in the blanket and turn on my side, pulling my hair back from under him. Pompon stands and walks over me again. He sits on my ribs and starts scratching my tee-shirt under the sheets.

'OK, OK, you win. I'm up!' I know kittens are nocturnal; it's pointless to resist. Five a.m. is not that bad; it gives me time to play with my new pet and to get ready for school while everyone is still asleep.

Pompon jumps off the bed and catches one of my white socks as if it were a mouse. Kittens need to play; they have a hunting instinct. I tie the sock to a string and drag it on the floor. My little fur ball pounces every time I move the sock. His legs are like mini springs: he lifts himself in the air and lands on its sock-prey with his front paws. I giggle in silence. No one must hear us. I tie more strings around paper balls and squishy toys for him to play with.

Before Mum and Dad wake up, I prepare fresh bowls of water and food for Pompon and change his litter box. I don't want the smell to alert them; it's a miracle already that Mum didn't notice Pompon last night.

Oh no! Now Pompon is scratching my carpet. Trouble ahead! I push him away gently, and, instead, I give him the cardboard montage I created for the geography class: a map of France with triangle blocks for the French Alps. I place it on the floor and point. Pompon stares at me, tilts his head, looks at the cardboard, and starts clawing the Alps. Good cat.

It's nearly time for breakfast. I go wash in the bathroom, put on my school uniform and take my school bag out of my room. With one final look around, I give a big cuddle to my baby cat, close the door tight and hang up a sign: **'Tempest's private space. Do not enter.'**

I'm eating my breakfast cereal when Mum comes into the kitchen to make coffee. Coffee's the most important thing in the world for Mum in the morning.

'Good morning, Tempest. You're up early!' She can be surprised: I always get up at the last minute to go to school; I hate alarm clocks and early rises.

'How's your tummy?' she asks.

'My tummy, why? Oh yes! Much better, thanks, Mum!' *Phew.* I had already forgotten my excuse from last night. I don't know how long I can hold on to this situation. I give myself two more days. If I can keep my secret for two more days, I'll show Mum and Dad that I can care for a pet all by myself and they will let me keep Pompon. I think. That's my plan. Today should be easy enough: Mum will take Wallace to school and then go to the office until after I come back from school. Dad will go to the office, and then he will take Wallace to football training after school. Both my parents will be busy and out of the house, which gives me a chance to hide Pompon safely for a bit longer.

After breakfast, I go and see my brother to explain that I've organised everything for Pompon. He only needs to watch that neither Mum nor Dad enters my room. Wallace promises.

I leave home feeling hopeful. In two days, I will tell the truth, and Pompon will be a new member of the family. I got this. Fingers crossed.

The morning is bright. I hop around on the street to wake myself up after the short night. Suddenly, I freeze: a silhouette I recognise in the backlight is walking towards me: baggy pants, a melting hat, and flat shoes sliding on the pavement. The mysterious old man with steely blue eyes is slowly approaching. *Who is he? Why is he looking at me again? What does he want from me?* I slow down my steps, holding my breath. My hands are sweaty, but I stare straight at him. I can defend myself. I'm strong.

Steely Blue gets closer. He lifts his head at me without a smile, nods slightly as if to say hello, and passes me without stopping. He looks around the street like he's searching for something, then turns a corner and disappears. This time, my tummy really aches.

Chapter 6
A shock

'*Finally!*' I whisper, keeping the smiley face of a good student. I thought Miss Watkins would never stop talking; we would have to stay at school all night, locked in the classroom by a crazy teacher. But, no, she stopped. My imagination was going wild again. People say I'm over-dramatic, but I'm just cautious.

Miss Watkins is our Geography teacher. She's nice, but she loves her topic so much that she keeps yapping about rivers and sand benches long after school time is over. When she finally says: 'That's it for today. Don't forget your revision for the test on Wednesday.' I pick up my bag and walk out of the classroom, taking the longest steps, looking at my shoes so no one talks to me. Once in the corridor, I take a sprint, my schoolbag bouncing on my back. I run past the giant poster that says: 'In hallways walk, don't run', I zigzag around the backpacks, pupils and teachers wandering slowly in the corridors and staircases. *Why is everyone always so slow? Don't these people have anywhere to be?*

I can't wait to be home. I've been thinking about Pompon all day; I couldn't concentrate on anything else. I didn't listen to Luna at break time telling me about her birthday party last weekend. Why would I? She didn't even invite me. But I don't care: I've found my best friend. I don't need pretend friendships. I trust the love I see in my cat's eyes more than any of these people. That's worth a thousand birthday parties.

I'm still running when I pass the pet shop near our street. The librarian-pet shopkeeper is standing behind the window, arranging a display of cat trees and toys. She lifts her head just as I pass by. Without slowing down, I wave at her and smile. I'll be one of her regular customers now.

I get home in nine minutes and twelve seconds, a personal best for me on that distance, including stops at the traffic lights. I catch my breath while looking for my keys. There's no one home yet:

Mum's still at work, and Dad and Wallace will come back only later from football training. I look forward to having Pompon all to myself, with no need to hide or stay silent. My hands shake with excitement when I put the key in the front door lock. I rush up to my room to hug my best friend.

'Pompon, it's me, Tempest. I'm coming, my baby,' I call from the staircase, excited to hold my little fur ball in my arms. He'll be so happy to see me. He must be playing or sleeping now, cuddled around my soft toys. I hope he did not spill his water or pee on my bed!

'My baby cat, I'm back' I continue, now at my bedroom door.

Oh no, no, no!! My heart sinks: the door sits unlatched, half open. I push it slowly with trembling hands.

'Pompon?' my baby's name strangles in my throat. I don't want to believe what I fear. *Maybe everything's alright.* Maybe Wallace came in and simply forgot to latch the door. Maybe Pompon is hiding behind the bed or in my soft toys, like last night. Maybe he's asleep under the bed or in my wardrobe. Maybe he slipped into one of my shoes like a little cubby house. Maybe he's still here.

Maybe I haven't lost my best friend.

I feel tears coming to my eyes. **No, no, no, it can't be!** I shouldn't panic; it will be ok. He cannot be far. I lie flat on the floor, flashing a light under the bed: nothing except two dusty old socks and one shoe. I pull away the piles of soft toys, the ones I used to love so much, searching madly while they stare at me with their plastic eyes, indifferent to my pain. I rip through my clothes, in my wardrobe, among my toys. I squat on the floor, holding my breath, listening to any noise that could signal Pompon's presence. This time, there's no scratch, no meow to break the silence.

In a frenzy, I run through the house, calling for my little cat. I open every door and check every room: Wallace's bedroom stinks like a football shoe forgotten overnight in a plastic bag. I push around the footballs, the softballs, the video games. From his poster on the wall, Lionel Messi looks at me as if to say: 'You won't find your cat here'.

Mum and Dad's bedroom is neat and tidy, a sign that Dad is back: Dad likes everything to be orderly. He made the bed square, like he used to do when he was in the army. No kitten there.

Cats don't like water, but I check the bathroom anyway: all is white, cold, and quiet.

Downstairs in the kitchen, I go through every cupboard and open every drawer. I look behind each cushion, under each piece of furniture in the living room. I'm not fighting my tears anymore; they roll onto my cheeks, dripping on the floor, leaving traces of sorrow everywhere I look for my baby cat.

'Pompon where are you?'

My question echoes through the empty house. My heart feels heavy as I sink onto the couch, weeping and discouraged. But it only lasts for a moment: *Tempest, pull yourself together* commands a voice inside of me. I need to calm down and think straight. Pompon is out there, maybe scared, maybe in danger. Someone has taken him, and it's up to me to figure out who. I will investigate and rescue my pet. Brave kids never give up. I stand up, determined. Wiping my tears with the back of my sleeve, I grab the house keys and slam the door behind me.

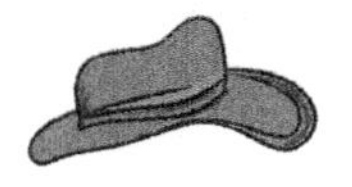

Chapter 7
Steely Blue

When I come out to the street, dark clouds are hiding the sun and a wind has picked up, blowing dead leaves onto the sidewalk. I am walking around slowly, searching for Pompon. Maybe he's hiding under a car, or behind a wall? I keep quiet, I don't call him; I don't want to attract the attention of people around me, but I remain on my guard. I decide to go back to the park. That's where I found my baby cat, so maybe that's where he will return. Animals often go back to familiar places.

The park is quiet. There's only a mother pushing a pram and the old granny with purple hair reading her favourite book. I cut through the grass to stand under Elmo. I stand still and listen, hoping to hear something, like a meow from above, like when it all started. It was only yesterday, but it feels like ages ago already.

While reflecting on what to do, I kick a pinecone that goes rolling far in front of me. It stops just before it hits the back of two old shoes looking like slippers at the bottom of a pair of baggy pants: Steely Blue! He's walking away from me, so I can only see his back. He slowly makes his way to the gate of the park, carrying a big tote bag with black and white drawings printed on it. The bag looks heavy and square as if there is a box in it. *What's in the bag? Why do I keep seeing this mysterious old man?* I must be careful; maybe he's evil. He hasn't seen me yet, and I have so many questions that I decide to trail him to find out more.

I have read guides on 'How to tail someone like a pro' in case I would need to do it one day. It's good to be prepared. To tail someone without being caught, you must stay at a minimum distance of ten meters, but not lose sight of your target. You need to adapt to the pace of the person you follow but blend into the environment so as not to get noticed. You should not do anything suspicious and look casual, like everyone else on the street. Deep breath. I got this.

Until we leave the park, I follow him at a distance, hiding behind the trees and flowering bushes. I don't want him to see me if he turns around: he could recognise me and hurt Pompon out of revenge if he's the one who snatched my baby cat. *Calm down, don't be dramatic again,* I tell myself. I must stay focused.

Following Steely Blue on the streets is harder than in the park because there are no bushes to hide behind and no crowd to blend into. I walk about ten meters away from him on the opposite sidewalk but always keeping him in sight. When he turns a corner, I accelerate. I stop when he stops and I walk when he walks, adapting to his pace. He's slow, so it's easy, but I need somewhere to hide. By chance, a woman who looks about Mum's age comes out, typing on her phone. She walks slowly, trying to type and walk at the same time. She's giving me the perfect cover in case Steely Blue turns around.

After two more turns, I can't recognise where we are. In front of me, Steely Blue takes a long, paved street that I haven't seen before. The wind carries a smell of wet sand and the noise of the old wooden boats cracking and clapping on the grey water.

The light changes. The river Thames opens wide in front of us. For a moment, I stand still, looking at the red sun, glaring through the dark clouds, reflecting on the glass buildings in the horizon.

While I was captured by the view, Steely Blue kept walking. When I look back at him, he's almost halfway across the river bridge, still carrying the bag. *Oh no! What is he doing over the river? Is he going to throw my baby cat over the bridge and drown him?* **No, no, no!**

I start running, the wind blowing in my face, sand and dust coming into my eyes. I don't know if my tears are coming from the wind, or from the terror of having my sweet kitten hurt by an evil man. I forget all prudence and run in the open, over the bridge. I must save Pompon!

But before I reach the top of the bridge, Steely Blue has continued on his way: he didn't empty his bag; he didn't throw my kitten over the bridge, nor did he see me. *Phew*. My imagination went wild again. I stop and lean forward, hands on my knees, to catch my breath and recover from my emotions. Steely Blue is still walking. I hide behind a pillar of the bridge, holding my two hands like binoculars to watch him.

The wind's still blowing strong, and the man holds his soft hat with one hand, so it doesn't fly off. He gets off the bridge and enters a tall glass building on the other side of the river, shining in the red sun. The glare on the big glass window blinds me. I need to get closer to investigate.

I run to hide in the dark stone staircase leading to the river bench from the street. Steely Blue can't see me from here: I'm hidden from the street, but I can watch the entrance of the building through the gaps of the staircase. I sit on a step and wait. I wait and wait. It's taking a long time. The stones are damp, and my bum is becoming wet. The sun has now set behind the buildings and I'm getting cold. This spy mission is more boring than I thought. *Is that what spies do: just wait in cold staircases with a wet bum?*

Just as I stand up to check what's happening, Steely Blue walks out of the big glass building. I squat down again quickly and watch, my eyes just over the wall edge. I hope that he won't see my big hair popping out. I notice he doesn't carry the bag anymore, and he looks tired. The mysterious old man pulls up the collar of his patched velvet jacket and starts walking back over the bridge with his sliding steps, leaning on his cane.

I come out of my hiding place to inspect the building after he's gone. It's a scary combination of light and dark. The front entrance is glassy and shiny, but the back of the building is made of old stones, turned black with pollution and time. It's like the building is showing off its front but hides some dark secrets in its back.

The front door is locked; you need a key card to get in. A name is engraved on a shiny metal plate: EQ Ltd. *Why would an old man like Steely Blue carry a heavy bag all this way?* It must be important. I want to find out, but I can't see through the glass walls. There must be another entrance, in the black rear of the building.

I leave the street and walk through the tall grass, around the building. The brambles cling on my socks and scratch my legs. Just as I'm about to find a way in, my phone vibrates in my skirt pocket, tickling my thigh. It's a text from Mum: **TEMPEST, WHERE ARE YOU?? COME HOME AT ONCE!!**

Chapter 8
Home detectives

Mum seems mad. And when Mum's mad, she screams so loud that even the neighbours get scared. Caught up in my investigation, I didn't look at the time; it's nearly 6.30 pm. Mum and Dad and Wallace must be all back home now. Oops.

I give the building a last look and promise myself to be back. I turn around in the brambles that scratch my bare legs even more: ouch! It hurts, but there is no time to cry; I must go home. Let's hope Mum and Dad won't ask too many questions. They can be very inquisitive when they decide to know something.

Back on the street, I start running as fast as I can. I'm still in my school uniform and my clunky leather shoes are giving me blisters, but I don't slow down. I'm stronger than that. I have more important things to worry about.

But just as I thought things couldn't get worse, I take a wrong turn. I was so busy earlier, following Steely Blue that I did not notice the way we went. I only remember the big, paved street leading to the Thames that I followed in reverse, but what was before that? What if I get lost?

My phone has just 5% of battery left, but that should be enough to follow the blue dot on the map to take me home. It's Mum's old phone and the battery goes flat very quickly. She gave it to me for my eleventh birthday 'for emergencies only'. This is an emergency! My pet is missing and Mum is mad. That's TWO emergencies.

I arrive home just eight minutes after Mum's text. It wasn't that far after all. I thought I had walked for ages, but that's probably because Steely Blue walked slowly.

'Tempest, thank God!!' shouts Mum, jumping out of her chair when she hears me coming through the door. She knocks her laptop off, and it lands on the carpet with a soft *thump*. Mum doesn't even look back at it and runs to me.

'Where have you been? I've been worried sick!

You almost gave me a heart attack!' She pulls me close to give me a big hug and I can feel her shaking a little bit. *Phew.* Mum's not so mad; she was just worried. Mum yells when she's scared, and only gets scared about us. For the rest, Mum fears nothing or no one; it's more like everyone fears her.

'Tempest, look at you! What's this mess? What have you been doing?' Mum stands back to look me up and down: I'm all sweaty, my uniform shirt is creased, half pulled out of my skirt, and my legs are all scratched. My hair looks like a big, tangled ball of fluff on my head, my hands are covered with dust, and there is dirt under my nails. Not a great look.

Mum faces me, arms crossed, waiting for an answer. I stand still, looking up at her, mouth open, arms hanging on each side of my skirt twisted to one side, incapable of finding an answer. *Think, Tempest, think! Say something quick!* shouts a voice inside of me, but I blank out. All I can think of is the shiny building with a dark back entrance, Steely Blue and his bag, and my missing kitten. *I can't tell that to Mum.*

'Baaaaabe, can you come here for a minute please?' shouts a voice from upstairs. *Phew.* Saved by the gong. The gong is Dad. He calls Mum like Wallace does, all the time, for all sorts of little and big things. Mum rolls her eyes, but she loves it. She turns around to go and see Dad, giving me a brief relief. I quickly go wash my hands, put my clothes back in place and try to comb my hair with my hands. If I look better, maybe I'll think better.

Wallace is in the kitchen, nibbling on a piece of cold pizza while playing with a soft ball.

'Wallace, help me find an excuse for Mum and Dad about where I was. Something happened—I'll explain later. For now, I can't tell the truth, and I can't think of a good excuse. Please give me an idea,' I ask my brother.

'But where were you?'

'I can't tell you right now. Invent something.'

'Hmmm... you've been kidnapped by aliens and taken on their spaceship,' he says with a big smile, proud of his idea.

'What??!!'

'Hum… you went to watch a football game?' my brother tries again.

'Not helping, Wallace,' I respond, disappointed. What was I thinking? Wallace is eight; of course, he likes spaceships and football. I'm the big sister; I should handle this. I bite on a piece of pizza, too. I don't want to go to my room and risk seeing Mum again. I just stand there, waiting for something helpful to happen.

Something happens. Mum and Dad come down the stairs as if they were walking on the red carpet of a movie premiere: Dad's wearing his tuxedo, and Mum, her silk red dress.

'Daddy!'

'Princess! I am so happy to see you!... Oh, dear! Where have you been to look like that? Be careful, Tempest! I don't want you on the streets alone after school time, you know that.' Dad looks at me suspiciously, but he's not mad; he's too happy to see me after a long trip.

'And you, Daddy, where have YOU been?' I ask to deflect the conversation and avoid answering his question.

'I was in Tokyo, the country of … Pikachu! And… Lucky cats!' says Daddy with a smile, pulling out toys from behind his back: a yellow Pikachu figurine for Wallace, and, for me, a "maneki-neko": a little cat figurine with an arm up that brings good luck. I gasp at the irony of the gift: *would it be a sign?* I so hope that my new good luck cat figurine will help bring back my real, beloved new kitten!

'Thank you so much, Daddy!' I say with all my heart. I don't want to make his tuxedo dirty by hugging him, so I blow kisses.

'Thank yoooouuuu Daddy!' repeats Wallace, 'I love Pikachuuuuu!' Then he adds, impressed: 'You guys look smaaaart.'

'Daddy and I are going to the opera tonight,' Mum explains. 'There's cooked pizza in the kitchen, with carrot sticks and cucumbers. Have a glass of milk with that. Be good.' Mum doesn't care about cooking or eating, so she thinks it's good enough when all the food groups are covered in a meal. The glass of milk is for protein, pizza for carbs and fats, and vegetables to stay healthy.

'Call Mrs Huntington if you need anything,' she continues, 'The monitors are on. Good evening, Mrs Huntington!'

'Have a lovely evening, Mrs Walker. Don't worry. The children and I will be fine.' says a voice on the baby monitor. Mrs Huntington is our next-door neighbour and occasional babysitter. Mum uses our old baby monitor between our house and Mrs

Huntington's, so our helpful neighbour can hear us if there's a problem.

'Bye Princess, bye my Best Buddy,' says Dad, giving us each a kiss on the forehead. Dad looks like he'd rather stay home with us instead, eating pizza and watching tele. He doesn't like opera, but Mum loves it, and Dad loves Mum, so he goes with her. I hope I won't have to do things I don't want to do when I grow up; it looks annoying. I don't want to get married anyway. Problem solved.

'Byyyyeee,' says Wallace to Mum and Dad, waving both hands. Then he turns to me and whispers: 'What's Opra?'

'Opera is like a theatre play, but where people sing loud for three hours.' I respond with a low voice, so Mum doesn't hear me.

'Oh, I see,' says Wallace, looking puzzled. I'm sure he doesn't see anything at all, but he drops it.

On the good side, it means that Wallace and I have the whole evening to investigate Pompon's disappearance and look for clues.

'OK, Watson,' I whisper to my brother, as soon as Mum and Dad have left, 'let's start our investigation.'

‘Why do you whisper? And why are you calling me Watson?’

‘I whisper because I don’t want Mrs Huntington to hear us, and you must keep your voice down too. Just say things out loud when you want Mrs Huntington to hear, like this,’ I murmur. Then I add, loud and clear:

‘Wallace, my dear brother, let’s go have a wash and put our pyjamas on. We must be clean for supper!’ I give my brother a big wink. Wallace giggles in silence, covering his mouth with both hands.

‘Something terrible happened,’ I explain, whispering in his ear, ‘Pompon is missing. Someone took him from my room. He might be in danger. We need to find him quick, or he could die!’ Wallace looks at me, hands still on his mouth, petrified. His eyes fill up with tears.

‘It’s an important case,’ I continue, trying to sound calm and encouraging, ‘I’m Sherlock Holmes, the great detective, and you are Dr Watson, my faithful companion. Together, we will solve Pompon’s mysterious case. We will save our cat.’ Watson nods. He understands. I stomp upstairs, followed by Wallace, holding Pikachu in his arms. I gently put the toys away. The investigation begins.

We start from the crime scene, which is my bedroom. I pull out latex gloves from my Sherlock Holmes box set for Watson: he shouldn't add his fingerprints to any exhibits. I don't need gloves; my fingerprints are all over my room anyway. I take the flashlight.

The litter box is untouched, but the food bowl is gone. One of the paper toys I made for Pompon is missing, too. Why would a villain take Pompon's food and toy? The carpet is not scratched, and there is no sign of struggle. It looks like the kidnapper did not want to hurt Pompon. *Why? Isn't he a bad guy?* We need to find out more.

'Watson, would you be so kind as to lend me your magnifying glass?' I ask my brother, talking with a deep voice. I'm sure Sherlock Holmes had a deep voice. I am dead worried, but I want my little brother to stay happy. I am his big sister, it's my responsibility to protect him and solve the mystery of Pompon's disappearance without Wallace being distressed.

I lost the magnifying glass of my detective set, but Wallace keeps one somewhere in his room. I can hear him emptying two drawers on the floor. He comes back running with the piece. 'Thank you, Watson.'

Up close, we can see tiny holes on the cardboard of the French Alps that Pompon used to claw this morning. There are little circle shapes, as if someone poked it with something…

'High heels!' says Watson, excited 'High heels like Manie's snake shoes.'

'Don't be ridiculous, Watson. It can't be Manie; she's our ally. Plus, Manie would never be able to look after a pet, she can't even keep a green plant alive! She'd never do this to us. She wouldn't. Surely.' I try to sound convincing, but my voice is fading. Watson can't be right. He can't be.

We follow the trail of poking marks leading outside of my room. They're hard to see; we're walking on hands and knees, looking through the magnifying glass. The marks on the carpet go down the stairs. Manie was here yesterday; she could have left the marks then. But not on the cardboard. I feel nauseous. We lose the trail on the marble of the entrance hall.

'Let's look under the furniture,' I whisper. 'Watson, take the flashlight.' My brother lies flat on the floor, looking under the buffet, the dust tickles his nose: **aaattchii, aaaatttcchhhiiiiii, AAAATTTCCHIIIIII!!!!**

'Kids, is everything OK? Do you want me to come over?' says the voice on the baby monitor.

'No, no, Mrs Huntington, that you very much,' I respond quickly. 'We're fine. There's no need to come, I assure you. Wallace just has a little cold. We will have our dinner now and go to bed. Good evening, Mrs Huntington.' I'm speaking with a high-pitched voice. I hope our neighbour doesn't know that's a sign I'm not telling the truth.

Watson sweeps the flashlight under the entrance buffet. He calls me with a sign of the hand to lie down next to him. 'There's something underneath, but I can't reach it,' he whispers. I stretch my arm under the big wooden drawers until my fingers find a small scratchy object. I pull it out.

'It looks like a mini toilet roll with spikes,' says my brother. 'Heehee! That must hurt your bum!' he giggles. Wallace can never be sad for long.

'It's not a toilet roll,' I say, not amused at all. 'It's a hair roller, like the ones Manie puts under her beret…' But then I suddenly think about it... Manie wasn't wearing a beret yesterday when she came to visit; that's not when she lost it. This must be more recent, like today. Could it be that Manie has taken Pompon? I can't believe it. How could she do this to me?

'Look, Tempest!' continues Watson, focused on the case, 'there's little white and black hair on the floor. These could be Pompon's, couldn't they?'

'Yes, Watson, probably. You're a good detective; well done. Let's go to bed now.'

Dinner is forgotten. I walk up to my room slowly. I feel like I weigh a ton, like a giant rock rests over my shoulders, crushing me. I hold the handrail with both hands not to fall. *How could she? Why?*

Alone in my bed, I try to gather my thoughts. There's no point calling my grandmother tonight; she never answers her phone anyway. It usually lies at the bottom of her bag or forgotten somewhere in her living room. I send her a text that I hope she will see before the morning: '**I MUST** see you after school tomorrow. Can you **PLEASE** come and pick me up with Wallace?'

I feel so tired and numb. I fall asleep, praying that Pompon is safe with Manie. *Please let us be reunited tomorrow.*

Chapter 9
Manie's place

'Good morning, Tempest,' says Mum when I come downstairs for breakfast. She's standing in the middle of the kitchen, holding her cup of coffee with both hands. 'Your grandmother called; she wants to pick you up from school. Would you like that?'

The good thing about Mum is that she lets us make as many decisions for ourselves as possible. Mum says she believes in self-determination—even for children—on matters that are big enough or small enough for them. That's why she asks.

'Yes, that's good, Mum,' I say, secretly relieved that Manie saw my text and agreed. 'I'll go with Wallace.'

On my way to school, I text Manie: 'Is Pompon safe with you?' I keep holding my phone in my hand all the way to school in case she responds. I wait and I wait. Manie finally texts back, just before I must put my phone in a locker for the day: 'I will see you at school pick up.' *That doesn't answer my question!*

I spend the day thinking about Pompon, wondering what Manie meant. She's hiding something from me, but I don't know what it is. In class, my mind wanders to my missing kitten and I can't focus.

'Tempest, do I need to repeat my question?' Miss Watkins wakes me up from my daydream. She wants to know which river goes through Paris. I'm sure she knows. *Don't ask me then!* I stare at the class clock all day as if I could make it go faster.

When the final bell rings at 4:15 pm, I'm the first out of the class, running down the stairs to join Wallace in the courtyard. Year 4 classes finish 15 minutes earlier than us. Standing at the school gate, we can see Manie's car far away. Only our grandmother drives a 20-year-old turquoise VW Beetle: 'Tempest of Provence'. Manie named her car after me. How embarrassing!

Beeep, Beeep, Beeep, she hits the horn really

loud, three times, as if we couldn't have seen her already. Everyone's staring at us; I want to disappear into the ground.

'Jump in, quick!' she shouts, slowing down in double park and opening the car's rear door. We rush into it. Manie presses the gas pedal before the school crossing guard reaches us. I shut the back door closed and Manie is already driving. In the back mirror, the man stands in the middle of the road, hands on the hips, staring at us with a dark look. Manie waves at him with an open hand, wriggling her fingers, her bracelets clicking with the move. I wonder if she's apologising to him or mocking the rules. Our grandmother always does what she wants.

'Manie, where's Pompon?' I ask, my voice cracking. There is nothing in the car; I was secretly hoping to see a cat carrier bag, but no. The giant hand is back, clenching my throat.

'Let's go home,' says my grandmother, avoiding the question again, 'I have scones, jam, and sugar bread for tea.'

'Yes! Yes! Sugar bread! **SU-GAR-BREAD!**' sings Wallace, bouncing on his seat like Tigger when he's excited.

All I can think of is my baby cat. Something's wrong. *Don't panic, Tempest, just breathe and wait to know,* I keep telling myself. But it's not working.

We arrive at Manie's in just a few minutes. I wait for my grandmother to unlock twice her heavy front door. Manie lives in a flat on the second floor, with a large terrace. She likes being outside, sitting in the sun and feeling the fresh air. She opens the big bay windows as soon as a ray of sunshine hits the glass, even in the middle of winter. Manie spends more time on her balcony than inside her flat.

My eyes sweep the living room, looking for my little fur ball. Lying at the bottom of an armchair, between the coffee table and the chimney, I spot one of the paper toys I made for him. I move forward to pick it up and I inspect the floor. There's cat hair on the carpet. Pompon was here. Where is he now? I walk to the kitchen. Pompon's food bowl sits on the floor, untouched. The scones and sugar bread on the kitchen table look at me, dry and cold. I'm not hungry.

'Manie, where's Pompon?' I ask again, with a faint voice.

'My sweetheart, I have to tell you something...'

'WHAT?' I scream now, and tears are coming to my eyes. 'What do you have to tell me, Manie? That you took my cat? I know that. I'm not stupid. I'm not a naive child who doesn't understand what's going on. I know you took him. I found evidence pointing at you all over our house last night and again here: the paper toy, the food bowl. He's my new best friend, and you took him away from me! Why Manie, why? Why would you do this to me? I thought you loved me; I thought I could trust you. Where is he now?'

Without waiting for Manie's answer, I run across the apartment, I open her bedroom door—the one she wants to keep private from everyone—and check under the bed. I step into the bathroom and the walk-in closet, pulling out the clothes from her suitcase left in a corner. I'm crying now. My hopes of finding Pompon crumble like a sandcastle hit by a giant wave.

'MANIE WHERE IS MY CAT?'

'Tempest, sweetheart, please sit down.' Manie speaks to me softly. That's very unusual for her. She takes me by the shoulders and walks with me back to the living room. 'Wallace, my big boy, go to the kitchen to have your snack if you like. The sugar bread is on the table.'

'Yes! Yes!' Wallace hops to the kitchen. Sugar bread is his favourite food, and Manie knows it. That will keep him distracted. I don't want Wallace to feel as sad as I do. Manie sits me down on her deep sofa and kneels in front of me. There's sadness in her eyes. She holds my hands in her hands; her bony fingers hurt a little, but I don't say anything.

'Sweetie, it's true, I took Pompon yesterday. But not to hurt you. To help you. I know my daughter—your mum. If she had found him and realised that you lied to her, she would have been furious at you. She would have forced you to give your cat away to teach you a lesson. Even after two days, even after many days of you managing Pompon on your own, your plan could not work. I took Pompon to protect him. And you.'

'You did?' I ask, a little flame of hope lighting up in my chest like a mini candle. 'You took Pompon to help me? To be nice?' I say with a tiny voice, wiping my tears with my hand.

'Of course, sweetheart, I would never want to hurt you, ever,' says Manie as if she has heard my thoughts. 'I brought Pompon back here yesterday morning, after I came to yours using my set of keys. I settled him with food, water, and a toy you made for him. I told him to be good and left to go for lunch with my friend Yvonne.'

I listen in silence to Manie's story. She continues, squeezing my hands harder. Her bony fingers hurt even more, but I keep quiet. I brace myself for bad news. Manie's green eyes look like little grapes, sweet and sad: 'That's not all, unfortunately. I need to tell you something more. When I came back home in the middle of the afternoon, your cat wasn't there anymore. Maybe I got distracted by a charming old man who talked to me on the street when I left… I looked everywhere—I promise you, darling—everywhere. I can't find Pompon, sweetie, I'm so sorry.'

That's exactly what I feared. Pompon is lost, and he's in danger. I sit there, stunned. Images run through my head: a black and white tote bag, a bridge over the Thames, a shiny and black building, an old man who spoke to Manie on the street…

'Steely Blue!' I shout, jumping off the deep sofa. 'It must be Steely Blue! Middle of the afternoon?

An old man, you said? That's not long before I saw him after school, carrying a big tote bag. He was bringing Pompon to a shiny and black factory. That must be it. Let's go Manie, let's go!'

'A shiny steely blue factory? What are you talking about, Tempest?' Manie looks at me dumbfounded, but I'm so adamant that she stands up and does what I ask. She owes me, anyway.

'Wallace, let's go!' I yell across the room to my brother, still in the kitchen.

'Wheeerssshhh?' he asks, peaking through the doorframe, his mouth full of sugar bread.

'To our park,' I say.

We must confront Steely Blue.

Chapter 10
In the park

Wallace and I climb into the back of Manie's old car. It's only a short drive to the park, thank God! There's not a minute to waste. On the way, I explain that Steely Blue is not a part of a shiny factory, but an old man with scary blue eyes. Manie listens to me with attention. She likes the idea of meeting a new mysterious man. Most men that Manie meets she finds charming. I don't!

I tell her how I trailed Steely Blue from the park to the factory over the river bridge. Wallace is listening, too, because I never had the chance to tell him the whole story. I'm clenching my seat, eager to meet our prime suspect. Maybe now we will finally solve the mystery and save Pompon. Our best chance to find Steely Blue is at the park next to our house: he was there yesterday, and I always see him nearby. I cross my fingers that he'll be there today. Manie parks the car on the street almost correctly this time; there's only one wheel on the sidewalk.

I spot the old man as soon as I push open the park gate. He's sitting in the distance on a wooden bench, his hand resting on a tote bag beside him. I cut through the grass to walk straight to the accused. Wallace is trotting on his little legs to follow my pace. He's shorter than me, but he's strong. If Steely Blue gives us trouble, my sturdy brother will defend us. Wallace puts on his angry look: frowning eyebrows, tight fists. I know Steely Blue is an old man, but you can never be too careful.

Manie's following us as best she can, lifting her feet high at each step. She's trying not to stain her purple velvet shoes and black leather pants with grass and mud. She looks like a heron tiptoeing on a hot plate.

Steely Blue watches us marching towards him, immobile. Only his blue eyes get a little wider as we approach him. We must look like a weird gang of unusual soldiers.

Manie says: 'Oh, is that him? Steely Blue? That's not the man I was talking to yesterday. He looks

charming. And those eyes, Tempest, you were right! Those eyes! They shine like sapphires, even in the distance.'

Wallace says: 'I think he looks sad.'

I disagree with them both. I think he looks suspicious, but I keep quiet. We're close now and Steely Blue could hear us. I stop right in front of him, back straight, hands on my hips, in the power posture I learned from Mum. If I do the same, maybe I'll feel as strong as her.

'Good afternoon, sir,' I start straight away, trying to stay polite and contain the rage I feel inside me, facing my archnemesis.

'Good afternoon, Tempest,' he replies with a gentle smile.

'How do you know my name?' I gasp. I wasn't expecting that. I cross my arms and wait for his answer.

'I heard your brother calling you last Sunday in the park when you were playing with a squirrel on the grass, not long before you climbed up that big tree,' he replies, pointing at Elmo with his wrinkled hand. 'You were so high that when I looked up, I was afraid you'd fall. You're a brave kid, Tempest, a very brave kid,' he says, as if he's talking to himself. Then he looks down and seems lost in his thoughts. I'm puzzled. This is not at all going to plan, but I'm on a mission to find my cat. I take a deep breath to reconcentrate.

'Yes, that's the day I saw you, too,' I continue, 'That's the day I rescued a kitten from Elmo's branches. Pompon is our baby cat. We saved him from that tree. We looked after him. Why did you kidnap our beloved pet?' I look straight into his blue eyes. I try to look scary, but I'm only crossing my arms so he doesn't see my hands shaking.

'Yes, where is our Pompon?' Wallace repeats in a strange, deep voice. Wallace wants to sound like

Dad when he's mad. 'We know you stole our baby cat.'

'**I STOLE your baby cat?**' The old man looks shocked, but then, a light shines in his blue eyes, like the Heart of the Ocean sapphire, and he asks: 'Did you happen to find a black kitten with a white paw and a white patch on the chest like a baby's bib?'

'**Whaaaaa!** That's him! That's Pompon! Oh, you've found the kitten belonging to my grandchildren! **That's wwwwooonderrrrrfull !!**' Manie cheers, raising her arms to the sky. For a moment, I think she'll hug Steely Blue, but luckily, she just smiles. Manie can't help herself; she wants to charm every gentleman she meets, especially when they have blue eyes like my granddad used to have.

But Steely Blue doesn't share our joy. He looks down as if he would find the answer in the grass. 'I wish I had,' he says.

'So… you didn't kidnap him?' I ask, suspecting the answer.

'**Kidnap him?** God, no! You have the completely wrong idea about me, Tempest.'

Steely Blue gets up, leans on his cane, puts back

his tote bag over his shoulder, and starts walking to the gate. He does look sad: Wallace was right. We just stand there, feeling stupid.

But after a few steps, the old man turns around to us and says, 'Follow me. I need to show you something.'

Chapter 11
Family

Steely Blue lives in a tall, red-brick building alongside the park. We follow him through the hallway then we climb in single file, up a narrow wooden staircase. I walk directly behind him, with Wallace following me, and Manie coming last. The old man walks up steadily, one step at a time, gripping the rail with one hand and leaning on his cane with the other.

None of us say a word, waiting for Steely Blue's big reveal. *Who is he?* If he didn't kidnap my kitten, but knows what he looks like, what's his connection to Pompon?

The mysterious man doesn't turn around to check if we're following him; he knows we're there. Manie's high heels click on the wood and Wallace hops from one leg to the other, and I tiptoe, trying to move as quietly as possible. I don't know what to expect. I am on high alert. I am always on high alert.

At the top of the stairs, Steely Blue pulls out a long key from the deep pocket of his old velvet jacket to unlock an old, squeaky door; the name tag says: **'Mr Quinn, Flat 2'**. He takes us through another narrow, shady corridor. Despite the obscurity, I can see framed drawings on the wall: angular figures, hairy dogs, a crocodile with an open mouth, thin trees growing to the sky... The corridor opens into a bright living room, lit by three large windows surrounding a fat wooden desk, though I can only guess there is a desk under the pile of papers, cardboards, canvases spread out all over it. Piles of drawings, notes, newspapers, and books sit around on the floor. On top of each pile are sketches in black and white or colour, of the same style as the frames in the corridor. The man looks just as messy as Manie and me. There's a smell of wax pencil and paper floating in the air, like at home when I draw and paint—but not only that: there's a smell like the smell in my room on Sunday when I was with Pompon.

'Tempeeessttt, loooook!' Wallace can't hide his excitement. I turn in his direction. In the back corner of the room, in a large fluffy basket, lies a beautiful black and white cat and three little black and white kittens snuggled against her belly. Wallace is already lying on the floor, petting the kittens' paws with the tip of his fingers, observed by their mother.

I stand still in the middle of the room, eyes wide, mouth open, incapable of a movement or a sound.

'Tempest, let me introduce you to Pompon's family,' says Steely Blue with a mischievous smile. 'That's what you call him, don't you?' he continues. 'It's a good name. I didn't have a name for him yet: he was number 4, and the others are—well, you can guess—number 1, 2 and 3. As you can see, I'm not very imaginative with names,' he says, still smiling.

'What's their mother called?' asks Wallace, lifting his head from the floor. I'm still too stunned to speak. I feel so stupid. I was so wrong.

'Duchess,' he responds.

'Like in the Aristocats,' I say, almost despite myself, without realising I'm even talking. The

Aristocats is my favourite Disney movie; I know all the scenes and songs by heart.

'I told you I wasn't very imaginative with names; my world is in images more than words.' Steely Blue gives me a wink: I think he's making fun of me a little. Worst of all, I deserve it.

'Who are you? What happened?' I manage to articulate.

‘My name is Eddie Quinn,’ says Steely Blue. ‘I'm a cartoonist. The drawings you see on the walls, on the floor, in those boxes: this is what I do. I draw to illustrate children's books, postcards, pictures, canvases, and even silk.’

‘Whaaaaa! Like me: I paint on silk, too!’ Manie exclaims. She's been so unusually silent so far that I'd almost forgotten she was here.

‘Really? How interesting,’ says Eddie Quinn, more out of politeness than actual interest. ‘I moved to the neighbourhood recently,’ he continues, ‘I needed to be close to my printing office and to live in a brighter place for my drawing. I'm an old man, Tempest, probably older than you imagine: my eyes are getting tired, and my legs too.’

‘So…’ I say, starting to put the pieces of the puzzle together, ‘the shiny and black factory over the river bridge, this is your printing office, isn't it? EQ Limited?’

‘Yes, you're right. EQ like Eddie Quinn, my company… but how do you know where it is and what it looks like?’

‘I trailed you there yesterday,’ I murmur, barely able to admit it out loud.

'You trailed me?' Eddie asks, his eyes narrowing in a smile. He's pretty amused with me now. 'Hahahaha, Tempest, you are a character. Why on earth did you trail me?'

'I thought you took Pompon from my bedroom and hid him in your big tote bag,' I say, blushing. I feel like hiding behind the curtains.

'My bag had only my drawings in it. A box of sketches I was bringing to be printed.... But hold on: your bedroom, you said? Was Pompon in your bedroom?'

It's time for me to tell Steely Blue—well, Eddie Quinn—the whole story. How Wallace found Pompon by nearly falling on him on the tree, how I hid him from Mum and Dad for fear they would get furious and force me to give it away, how Manie took Pompon to protect me from their reaction, then went out for lunch and lost him, and how I thought HE was the one who did it. But it's a dead end: our beloved kitten is still missing, and time is running out.

'I see. You're a courageous kid, Tempest, passionate and imaginative. I know you mean well,' says Eddie, 'Now, let me tell you my side of the story. When I saw you up that tree two days ago, I had just lost Pompon, but I hadn't realised it then. I was coming back from my daily walk in the park. At my age, I need to walk every day otherwise I would fossilise like a dinosaur. I noticed you so high up. I was impressed by how a tiny little girl like you would have the courage to climb so high. I spotted your big hair, like a lion's mane, before I saw your angry eyes looking at me. You look like a little fierce lion, Tempest; do you know that? You wear your name well. When I came back home that day, Pompon was missing. Since you found him in that tree, I can only guess he followed me to the park somehow without me noticing.'

'Oh…' I say, thinking at a thousand miles an hour, trying to make sense of the new information, and ignoring Eddie's comments about my lion mane or how courageous I am, or anything that has nothing to do with finding Pompon.

'So,' I say again, trying to save time to think, 'the last thing we know is that Pompon was at Manie's. She left for lunch, he's gone missing, and you did not kidnap him.'

'That's right,' Eddie confirms.

'So, he must still be there somewhere,' I say.

‘That's right,’ Eddie says again. They're all looking at me now: Eddie, Manie, Wallace, even Duchess, whose cat’s eyes seem to ask: ‘Will you find my baby boy, Tempest?’

‘Alright then,’ I say, ‘I need to go to Manie's and look around again, but differently. Who's coming?’ Silence. *Not everybody at the same time, please.*

‘Tempest, is it OK if I stay here for a little while to play with the kittens?’ asks Wallace.

‘My sweetheart, I looked everywhere. I can't find him. I don't think he's there anymore,’ says Manie. ‘Why don't I stay with Mr Quinn? We can talk about silk painting and wait here in case Pompon finds his way back home.’

I see. I'll need to do this on my own.

‘Whatever. If you want, Manie. I'll go. Give me the keys to your flat, please.’

‘If someone can do it, Tempest, it's you,’ says my grandmother with a large smile while passing me the keys. That's flattery; she thinks she can fool me, but she's doesn’t.

‘Thanks, I know,’ I say without responding to her smile.

‘Mr Quinn, may I please have one of Duchess's blankets? I'm sure the smell of his mother would help Pompon find his way back and comfort him. At that age, he already has an excellent sense of smell.'

'Of course, that's an excellent idea, Tempest. Good luck, my dear, and thank you. Please keep us updated. If we don't hear from you soon, we will ask for help.'

'OK, but not just yet, please, let me try first. Thank you, sir.' I close the flat door behind me. **I got this.**

Chapter 12
Think like a cat

I run down the narrow staircase out onto the street. If I keep running all the way, I can be at Manie's in ten minutes. **My kitten is in danger;** I sense it. Kittens that age can't survive more than two days without food and water, especially outside and in the cold. I must find him before it gets dark today. I accelerate. The Taekwondo training that Dad has made me do for years is handy for good cardio. Next year, I'll be a black belt. Still sprinting, I try to collect all my vet knowledge. I must think like a cat. What did Pompon do? He escaped to the park all by himself, sneaking out without anyone noticing. My curious, adventurous kitten has probably done the same at Manie's. *Gosh, where did he go? What are my chances of finding him?* I hold tight onto Duchess's blanket: it's my best hope to bring back Pompon.

I catch my breath while opening Manie's double-locked door. What was I thinking? It would have been impossible for Steely Blue to come here and kidnap Pompon with those locks. There is no chance for anyone to sneak in if Manie isn't there. Pompon must have escaped all by himself. Did he follow her to lunch? I inspect the flat entrance, the marble hallway, and the front door mat. I'm walking on all fours to be closer to the ground, using my phone as a flashlight to see better. I look like Mum when she can't read the menu at a restaurant.

There is no trace of Pompon outside Manie's flat: no paw prints, no little cat hair on the floor. That's reassuring; he might still be in the flat. But what are my chances if Manie hasn't found him already? Still crawling on my hands and knees, I look for scratch signs: Manie did not use a cardboard for Pompon to claw, so he might have used the furniture instead. Lol! I'm sure Manie would HATE that!

I follow the trails in the living room: tiny scratches on the carpet, a couple of missing and broken threads on Manie's Oriental rug, and some hair near the paper ball toy I saw earlier today.

Would he have climbed up the chimney?

I step into the unused fireplace and slowly stand up, sliding into the black chimney conduit. Holding my phone in front of my face, I look up. No kitten hidden there, but a ball of soot detaches and falls on my forehead. Great! Now I don't only look like a broomstick upside down; I look like a chimney sweep, too!

The chimney is a dead end anyway: why would Pompon go up a black chimney corridor full of soot? I must stop and think for a minute. I wipe the soot as best I can and sit cross-legged on the floor, like Mum when she tries to calm down and meditate to think more clearly. My back to the chimney, I observe the place around me: the locked entrance door, the corridor leading to Manie's bedroom and bathroom, both with their door closed, the kitchen with the food bowl untouched, the bay windows opening to the terrace… of course! The terrace! It's **SO obvious** now. Manie leaves these windows ajar all day, even sometimes when she leaves the house. Pompon must have wandered onto the terrace. Could he still be out there?

Holding my breath, I tiptoe to the terrace, full of hope. I open the bay windows and explore every inch of the terrace. It's quickly done: Manie's terrace is bare, designed more like a solarium than a green space: a reclining chair facing south, a mug forgotten on a coffee table, and two pots with shrunken plants dying from lack of water. It's a sad environment for a kitten. No wonder Pompon escaped. But where could he go?

The balustrade of the terrace starts at around ten centimeters from the tiles—quite enough for a kitten to get under. Oh God, no! I approach the rail, holding it with both hands to lean over. I'm terrified of what I might see down there.

One floor below, there is another terrace, only slightly larger than Manie's but looking very different: no reclining chair, no coffee table, only nature and colours. The entire surface is taken up by plants and flowerpots, surrounded by mint and lavender bushes. It's beautiful. I can't see the little body of my kitten on the tiles between the pots, thank God! If Pompon fell, he must have landed in one of the lavender bushes, those purple, high grass-like plants. Their lovely smell is mounting towards me from the green terrace. There's my hope! Pompon must be in the bushes: cats love the scent of lavender and mint; that's what must have attracted him!

I can't wait to go down and get him, fast! Poor baby must be so hungry and thirsty; maybe he's injured. There's not a second to waste! What if I jump? I'm tempted. I'm light: I could land in the bushes without too much harm. I'll do that. I climb over the balustrade, holding the bars with both hands behind my back. I look down: I must be at least ten feet off the ground, the height of a building floor. *Oh, Gosh, that looks quite scary now.* Maybe I shouldn't do this. If I break a leg, who will find me here? Worse, what if I fall on Pompon and hurt him? Oh, God! Jumping was a terrible idea. I must go back inside and ask to go through the downstairs neighbour's apartment instead. It must be his or her terrace. Manie always talks about her 'horrible neighbour', but she doesn't say why. I don't even know if it's a man or a woman. If I need to face a horrible neighbour, I'll do it. It's better than plunging down ten feet and risking landing on my poor cat with a broken leg.

I must come back inside. I let go of one of my hands off the rail to turn around; I need to pivot on the ledge. As I turn around to face the flat with one foot in the air, my other foot slips: it's my damn, horrible, slippery uniform shoes! Aaaaargggghhh! Now, I am hanging off Manie's balcony with just one hand. **How do I get out of this?**

Chapter 13
Lady Lavender

Come on, Tempest! Time to use these Taekwondo skills: I quickly grab the rail with my other hand and give myself a big side-swing to put one foot back on the ledge. *Phew!* Almost back to safety: I can now stabilise myself with my other foot on the side of the balcony, two hands on the railing, and climb over it to get back inside Manie's terrace. That was close! Dad would be proud of me for my strength and very mad, too, for the dangerous situation I put myself in. Talking about dangerous situations: it's time to face the horrible neighbour.

There's only one flat on the ground floor. Its black front door has no name tag, only a shiny silver knocker. I lean against the thick door to listen; there's only silence. I knock gently on the door, hoping to hear steps coming, but instead: **WHACK!** The noise of an axe hitting wood. I freeze in horror, all my senses on alert. **WHACK!** I jump back; I'm brave but not suicidal. I keep standing there, petrified, holding on to Duchess's blanket, ready to fight or fly. Suddenly, horrible shrieking and screaming noises mount from inside the flat. Alert! There's an axe murderer behind this door! I must stop him! With all my might, I swing the knocker and shout: **'OPEN THIS DOOR IMMEDIATELY!!'**

'Ohohoh, OK, OK, I'm coming! Just a minute!' replies a frail voice. There are hurrying steps, and the door opens to reveal a tiny old lady. She's barely taller than me, dressed all in green: green shoes, green socks, green dress. She even wears a little green hat on her light purple coloured hair. The tiny old lady smiles at me with purple eyes, circled by tiny wrinkles on her powdered skin. She smells of mint and lavender. She smells the same as she looks. I stand there, mouth open, my heart pounding in my chest, staring at a sweet old lady smiling at me with her lavender eyes.

'Oh, hello there!' she says, 'I am sorry if I kept you waiting. Would you like to come in?' I nod, muted. Lady Lavender precedes me inside, trotting on her bendy legs. She looks like a toddling green plant.

'I didn't hear you before, young lady; I can't hear very well anymore. Since you're here, dear, would you be so kind as to do me a favour? Could you please find the remote control and turn off the television for me? My grandson came and watched it earlier today, but he left it on blasting. These noises are just horrible.'

'Of course, ma'am,' I answer with a huge sigh. The tiny entrance hall opens to a living room that looks like a greenhouse: green plants and flowerpots cover all wooden furniture. Purple rose bushes surround an old television sitting on an antique buffet, facing a lilac sofa. I quickly find the remote control, fallen between the velvety cushions. I'm happy to switch off the horror movie that was playing. What a careless grandson to such a sweet grandmother!

WHACK! *That noise again! She's not a sweet grandmother; she's a murderer in disguise, and this was a trap. She'll kill me.* I turn around slowly, ready to face my fate. The old lady is standing in front of the kitchen, holding a long butcher knife.

‘Would you care to share some lamb chops with me, dear? I’m preparing dinner,’ she says. I gape. My paranoia got me again. On the kitchen bench lies a lamb rack chopped in slices, a fresh bouquet of mint, and potatoes ready to be roasted. I feel so hungry. Lady Lavender is smiling at me. She looks sweet. And lonely.

‘I would love to, too, ma’am. Thank you very much,’ I answer, as politely as I can. ‘However, before I do, may I please have a look on your terrace? I lost my kitten, and...’

‘Good Lord!’ she exclaims before I could finish, ‘Why didn’t you say so?’ Lady Lavender drops her knife and hurries towards the terrace as quickly as her legs allow her to. I follow right behind her, full of hope.

As we trot along, I quickly explain who Pompon is and why I think he fell on her terrace. Lady Lavender understands. She knows that cats love the scent of mint and lavender. She used to own cats when she was younger. They loved to hide in lavender bushes, she says. It was a reassuring, cosy place for them. These plants are good pollinators that attract bees and butterflies to help the flowers grow. Bees are buzzing around;

there are dozens of them. They're quite loud and scary. I don't want to get stung, but I'm anxious to find my poor kitten. It's been a long and rough day. I'm still shaken by my near fall earlier and the frightening noises behind the door, though I know I feared for nothing, once again.

Lady Lavender's terrace is a beautiful place of flowers, scents, and colours. We look among the flowerpots, between the plants, and through the bushes. I call my best friend softly: 'Pompon, Pompon, we're here my baby, you're safe now.'

'Young lady, come over here, please.' My heart stops: Lady Lavender is leaning over a lavender bush, her hands parting the tall stems. I leap up to join her and stare into the place where she is looking. **Pompon!!** My kitten is there, curled between the stems. He looks asleep. I pick him up carefully with both hands and I carry him in my arms like a tiny baby. He's still asleep. I look up at Lady Lavender as if to ask her what to do.

'Let's go back inside,' she only says.

I lay Pompon on the lilac sofa, and I wrap him in his Duchess's blanket. I give him a gentle pet: 'Pompon, wake up! It's me, Tempest!' No answer.

Now, I'm rocking him a little more firmly: 'Pompon! Pompon!' No movement.

Oh, no, no, no! No! Please, God. No!

Chapter 14
Pompon

Meow! Meow! Ouch! *Stop shaking me so vigorously Tempest, my dear, I am in such pain! I understand you fear for me, but I assure you I am alive. I cannot speak out loud to tell you this, but I do hope you will read my thoughts. I shall move, ever so gently, so you can understand. Just give me a moment, please; I am too feeble to open my eyes just yet.*

What an astonishing fall that was! I plummeted from such a height, and I have not yet mastered the art of rotating mid-air to land gracefully on all four paws, like an adult cat. Instead, I plunged headfirst into the bushes and, quite expectedly, lost consciousness.

I had no intention of embarking on such an extraordinary adventure—I merely wanted to explore the park outside of Eddie's flat for a brief moment. My sisters were utterly rude, teasing me constantly or chatting between themselves, ignoring me. **Ladies, pfff!** *Though, of course, I do not mean you, Tempest; you are the most delightful lady I have ever known. Well, you and my dear Mother Duchess, naturally.*

I thought that a firm demonstration of my bravery would end my sisters' mockery. As young kittens, we have never been outside of Eddie's apartment. My sisters did not care, but I longed for adventures, gazing out the window, observing the park with people wandering the alleys, squirrels running through bushes and birds chirping on tree branches. It was most tempting.

I carefully organised my escape for Sunday. The weather was splendid, mild and bright. A gentle breeze rustling the leaves on the park trees. I felt gorgeous; today was my day, or so I thought... **Pfff! Foolish, foolish me!** *If only I had known!*

I slipped into one of the large pockets of Eddie's jacket, just as he announced he was going to the park. Eddie wears his jacket every time he steps outside, even on mild days. I clung tightly as he put it on, gripping the fabric with my claws ever so firmly. Eddie dropped the heavy flat key in his pocket, which struck me on the head: ouch! But I made every effort to keep silent, and he did not notice me.

Just as Eddie sat on a park bench, I tiptoed out of the pocket and began my exploration. A grey squirrel darted up the grand tree in the middle of the park. I pursued him. Climbing up a real tree trunk was exhilarating! Unlike the toy cat tree in Eddie's apartment, I could claw at its bark, feeling ever so splendid.

Though soon the squirrel became too fast for me. I lost sight of him and sat on a branch to rest for a moment. From my point of observation, I saw Eddie walking out of the park. Excuse me! Excuse me!! Eddie! Come back!! Please do not leave me here on my own! **MEOW! MEEOOOWWWW!** *I called him with all my might, but he could not hear.*

Instead, you heard me Tempest and saved me for the first time. You climbed up the branches so swiftly, that you passed me right by without noticing me. Wallace nearly frightened me out of my fur when he fell right next to me!

Pompon is a lovely name; thank you ever so much. I had a delightful time with you and

Wallace, and you took such excellent care of me, Tempest. However, I could not quite explain my need to return to Mother. She must be dreadfully worried about me, and I miss her terribly.

On the first night in your bedroom, I attempted to find a secret tunnel passage to return home. Instead, I found myself trapped behind your bed frame. Twice in one day! How terribly embarrassing! Thankfully, you rescued me once again; you truly have a remarkable talent for finding me, Tempest. Sleeping against your chest, like I do with Mother, was a delight. The other animals on your bed were fixing me with unmoving eyes. It was mildly unnerving.

In the morning, I followed your instructions and remained perfectly quiet in your bedroom—until that strange old woman entered and seized me with her bony fingers. I hissed 'Pffff, pffff, pffff' to express my displeasure: 'Go away! Go away! I do not want you!' But she took me regardless. She could not even hold me properly: I dangled awkwardly in the air, bent over her meagre hands that gripped me far too tightly. And her scent, oh, it was dreadful! Her perfume made me quite nauseous. I believe I may have, ahem, slightly vomited on her.

Her flat was utterly dull. As I explored, I discovered a large walk-in closet with a suitcase tucked away in a corner, filled with shiny clothes and a puffy golden jacket. I jumped into it to play, but that horrid woman pulled me away and slammed the door shut. Pfff!

In the kitchen, she presented me with a bowl of dry food from the previous day—how disgusting! I refused to eat, though I am so terribly hungry now! I am famished.

That dreadful smell lingered everywhere. She claimed it was Patchouli: well, **I DETEST** Patchouli then. She sprayed more of it on her pink jacket and left to meet a friend, she said. The woman waved goodbye and told me to be good. Oh, I will be good! I will be out of here! Fortunately, the windows to the terrace were open enough at the top for me to climb onto the armchair, leap through, and slide down the window onto the terrace. **Hurray!** I was outside and free. I could finally return to Mother.

Except that I was not on the ground floor: I was as high up as the grand tree from the park. The terrace was bare and depressing. I jumped onto the long chair and lay in the sun for a few minutes. There was no food, and I was hungry.

I felt trapped once again! I was on the verge of tears when I caught the most delightful scent—a blend of mint and lavender mounting from below. I stepped under the railing, leaning over to catch a better whiff of the aroma. I took another step, slipped… and landed headfirst into the purple bush of the terrace below.

When I awoke, it was dark and cold, with no one around. It was terrifying. I was trapped in those tall stems like a prisoner. I feared no one would ever find me. I thought I might perish here, all alone. But you found me, Tempest, once again! You are my hero. You are my dearest friend, Tempest. You think like a cat.

But I miss Mother.

Why does it smell like Mother here?

It feels warm and cosy.

Did you bring Mother back to me, Tempest?

It has been so terribly long since I saw her.

I should never have left Mother.

Will you save me, Tempest?

I need water and food… and Mother.

Can you read my thoughts?

I don't have much strength left…

Chapter 15
Cat care

I gently palpate Pompon's whole body to check if he's injured. He looks knocked out, but his neck is not broken. None of his bones seem to be either. Kittens' bones are quite soft: even from that height, he may not have broken anything. The plants would have softened his fall. I put two fingers on his chest: there's a faint heartbeat: he's alive, Yay! But for how long?

Lady Lavender says, 'He's cold and must be very thirsty. Can you imagine going more than a day without water? Wrap him well in his blanket, my dear. I will get him some water.'

She returns from the kitchen, holding a tiny baby bottle filled with cloudy water.

'Here,' she says, 'I still had a bottle from when I used to feed my young kittens. You can give him some sugar water, like this. It will give him some energy and help him wake up.' Lady Lavender knows loads about cats—more than me. She's so nice. Why did Manie say her neighbour was horrible? That's another puzzle to solve later.

For now, I have my best friend to care for. I place the bottle's teat into Pompon's mouth. He's still young enough to have a sucking reflex and drinks it in a few gulps. He needed it! I wait, I watch, keeping him wrapped and warm in his Mummy's blanket, praying he'll be fine. Slowly, little ripples form on the blanket under my hands: Pompon starts moving a little. I feel his tiny body rolling and stretching. He turns his head from side to side, and he opens his eyes just halfway. Pompon looks at me and manages a *meeeooowww*, hardly audible. He's back with us! He's still weak and fragile, but my baby cat is back!

As soon as I hear my best friend's voice, it's as if a dam breaks inside of me. I burst into tears, kneeling on the floor, my head between my arms, buried in the sofa cushions. I sob, and I hiccup, unable to stop. There's been so much happening in so little time. I've been so scared.

Lady Lavender puts her arm around me and helps me off the floor.

'It's OK, young lady,' she says, 'You did it: you found your cat; you saved him. Rest now.' I'm so tired suddenly, as exhausted as Pompon. I lie on the sofa alongside him, my arm around his tiny body. I want to rest just for a minute, just for the time needed to dry my tears and get my strength back, because the day is not over yet.

Lady Lavender trots to the kitchen. She comes back with lavender tea and mint chocolate chip ice cream. Wow! Mint chocolate chip is my favourite ice cream flavour in the whole world, though I have only had it once before. Lady Lavender is like a magician.

'Here you go,' she says. 'Eat this, drink that, and you'll feel better in a minute. I'll keep feeding Pompon in the meantime. Then, we will bring him back to where he belongs.'

By the time I finish my ice cream and my tea, my kitten's eyes are fully opened. He looks better. He's moving slowly, turning his head to look at me, at Lady Lavender, and the room around him. Then he takes a big stretch, extending his front legs out of the blanket which makes us laugh.

'I think he needs to go back to his Mummy now,' I say, standing up with regret. I don't want to be separated from my best friend, but I know he needs his Mummy-cat for now.

'That's right,' says Lady Lavender. 'Young lady, if you have this blanket, I assume you know where Pompon lives?' I nod.

'Then we are on our way,' says Lady Lavender, putting on a green coat over her green dress and adjusting her green hat. 'Let's go, my dear.'

She insists on walking back with me to Eddie's place to look after me and to meet Pompon's family. I walk slowly, holding Pompon in my arms, still wrapped in the blanket, as if he were as fragile as crystal. It's good because Lady Lavender walks slowly, too. It takes us a little while to arrive at Eddie's at that pace, which is fortunate: it gives me a few more precious moments with my beloved kitten. I want Pompon to feel better and be happy, even if it means I must leave him with his Mummy. *I love him, and loving someone means wanting what's best for him.*

Silent tears roll down my cheeks. The giant hand grabs my throat again. I force myself to breathe just enough to carry Pompon up the stairs to Eddie's flat.

I ring the doorbell.

Chapter 16
Duchess

Eddie opens the door. 'Oh!' he simply says, his blue eyes widening from the happy surprise. A big smile spreads across his old face. He steps aside to let me pass through the narrow corridor leading to the living room. I walk carefully, holding my baby cat, who has fallen asleep again.

Wallace comes running towards me at full speed: 'Tempest, Tempest! Did you find Pompon?' He yells as if I'm very far away.

'STOP!' I extend my arm in front of me to protect my precious parcel. Wallace piles right in front of my hand. He could have banged me and squished Pompon by accident.

'Ooohhhh, is he sick??' Wallace's eyes fill up with tears at the sight of our sweet kitten looking unconscious.

'He'll be fine. You watch,' I say to reassure him. I hope I'm right…

In the living room, Manie stands up when she hears me coming: **'Whaaaaa Tempest! My champion! You did it; you found him; that's woonndderfullll!'**

I let her speak and kneel in front of Duchess, still in the big basket. I present her Pompon asleep, wrapped in her blanket and the mother cat looks up to me. Her eyes say: 'Thank you.' Inside of me, my heart smiles. I gently unwrap Pompon and lay him against her belly. Pompon's three sisters make room for him in the basket, but all of them stay close by, curious to witness the return of their adventurous brother.

Duchess looks at Pompon; she gives him a little knock with her snout, and starts licking him, slowly but firmly. She's showing her son that Mum is here, and that he's safe now. She licks the top of his head, between the ears, his face, his mouth, and his nose, to help him breathe and wake up.

'Oh. Hello, hum…. Mrs Simons.' Manie's cold, stiff voice takes me out of my contemplation of the cats.

'Good afternoon, Mrs Fagnart,' replies Lady

Lavender with a pinched voice I haven't heard her use before.

Eddie gently steers Lady Lavender away from the scene to show her his drawings. I step closer to Manie.

'Why did you say she was a horrible neighbour?' I whisper, 'She's only been nice to me and to Pompon.'

'Have you even looked at her?' my grandmother snaps. 'All dressed in green, from tip to toe! Wearing green brings bad luck! Worse, she knitted a horrible cardigan for my birthday: slimy green, large and loose. She called me and said out loud in the staircase: 'Happy 70th birthday, Mrs Fagnart!' Can you believe it? Yelling my age for everyone to hear? And cardigans are for OLD people. She wanted to humiliate me!'

'Manie,' I say, 'you ARE old. I know you don't believe you're old, but at 70, you are. She did not mean to offend you. Only you think wearing green brings bad luck! She doesn't: she loves green; everything is green around her, in her flat, on her terrace. It doesn't bring her bad luck.' Manie's fun and eccentric, but she can be unfriendly sometimes.

'Hmmm.' Manie's sulking. She's quite comical

when she's like that.

'Come on, Manie, be nice! At least do it for me: Mrs Simons helped me save Pompon, she cared for him and came back with me all the way here.' Manie stands still, arms crossed, lips tights while I lecture her, trying not to laugh. She looks like a moody kid. Adults remain just like kids inside, I suppose.

Thanks to his mother's care, Pompon is awake. He's purring lightly at first, then stronger and stronger. **'Meeeoooow, meeeeoooow'**, 'Hello Mummy,' his eyes say in his cute, happy face. My heart melts with love. But at the same time, I feel like a rock in my stomach: we will be separated again. I know it's for his own good; he's been through so much. He's home now, where he should be.

'Ah! It looks like our adventurous little boy is back to life,' says Eddie, walking back to the living room. 'Well done, Tempest! This is all thanks to you! Now, please tell us what happened; I am curious to know.'

I explain my search, how I almost fell off the balcony, and Lady Lavender's help to bring Pompon back to consciousness. When I finish my story, Pompon gets up and walks to me, purring.

He lifts his tail and rubs his back against my leg: a sign of love and friendship from cats. Pompon and I are totally best friends!

Everyone smiles and claps. Manie hugs Eddie with enthusiasm. Then, turning to Lady Lavender, she says: 'Well, I guess I was wrong about you. You did well for my granddaughter, thank you.' That's Manie's way of apologising—she never says 'I'm sorry.' Instead, she softens and moves on.

'You're welcome,' replies Lady Lavender politely, 'your granddaughter is a fine young lady.'

Wallace looks at us around the room: Manie, Eddie, Lady Lavender, me and him. **'Looooookkk! We're like the famous fiiiiiiiive!'** he shouts.

Everyone laughs.

'And Pompon is Timmy,' Eddie adds with a wink.

It's that perfect moment; everyone's happy, everything comes together, like at the end of a children's book… It gives me an idea.

'Mr Quinn,' I ask, 'would you draw our story?'

The old man looks at me, thinking. He looks at his pictures on the wall, on the desk, and smiles: 'Maybe, Tempest, maybe I could. If you write the story, I will illustrate it.'

I nod. It's a plan.

Something vibrates in Manie's bag, breaking the charm of the ideal moment.

'Manie, your phone's ringing,' I say.

'What did you say?'

'Your phone, in your bag!'

Manie hands her bag to me with a look that means: 'You pick it up.' *Why can't grown-ups ever find their phone or answer it in time?*

Manie's handbag is a big, messy sack. I pull out

two hair rolls, a pink lipstick, a mini perfume spray, a notepad, a wallet, keys, mints, and, finally, her phone. Success! I raise it victoriously, the phone still buzzing. My smile vanishes at the name on the screen. I plunk it in her hands.

'**You take it,**' I say.

Chapter 17
Coming clean

It's Mum calling. She hasn't heard from us in a while, and she's worried no one's home so late after school. With everything that's been happening, I had completely forgotten to text her.

Worse, Mum has found Pompon's litterbox under my desk. She's not happy and demands an explanation. *Oh God!*

After she has hung up, Manie turns to us and says: 'My dear children, now is the time to come clean to your parents.'

Wallace starts crying. I swallow with pain.

'Mr Quinn,' Manie says, 'I have been delighted to meet you. Mrs Simons, thank you for all your help with my granddaughter and the kitten.' Our grandmother is already walking us out of Mr Quinn's, her arms wrapped around our shoulders.

As I am about to step into the shady corridor, I turn around and ask: 'Mr Quinn?'

'Yes, my dear?' says Eddie, with his usual gentle voice.

'Are you going to keep all the cats?'

'Only for now. The kittens must stay with their mother for another two or three weeks. After that time, they will be ready to be adopted by a new family.'

'Oh,' I say, a little candle of hope lighting up inside of me. 'Would I be able to adopt Pompon, then? As his new family?'

'Yes, Tempest, I'm sure Pompon would like that. But what about your parents?' asks Eddie with a doubtful look.

'Hmmm, I don't know. But I'll ask.' I say, determined.

'You never give up Tempest, do you?' Manie says, rolling her eyes.

'No, I don't.'

'One thing at a time, let's go now,' ends Manie, leading us out of the apartment.

We walk back home slowly. Wallace squeezes my hand really hard. I force myself to breathe calmly, but I'm shaking. Manie leaves us at the front door.

'Off you go,' she says.

'Manie, come with us, please! You could explain to Mum what happened,' I beg my grandmother.

'No, Tempest, you can do this on your own,' she replies in a firm voice.

'But Manie, you took the cat!' I argue. It's not fair. She has her share of responsibility, too. *How dare she leave me hanging like this?*

'I will have my own conversation with my daughter, darling, I promise. But now is the time for you to face the consequences of your actions, good and bad. You can do this. You're the strongest, bravest, smartest young girl I know, and you will make things right, all by yourself.'

It's true that I am strong and brave and sometimes smart, but I suspect Manie is using flattery to get herself out of a difficult conversation—and it works.

Mum's waiting for us, standing in the hallway, arms crossed. Wallace's lips are trembling. I walk slowly. I'm too scared to look Mum in the eyes.

'You two, in the kitchen, please,' Mum simply says. She sits us down around the kitchen table, just like she did last Sunday after the chocolate incident. Though now, the lie is much bigger. We're back where we were two days ago, except that so much has happened since then. I feel different. I have come back to the same place, but I'm higher. 'Life is not a circle, it's a spiral,' Grandpa used to say; he liked ancient Asian philosophy.

Mum looks straight at us and just asks: 'What happened?' and waits.

I tell Mum the whole story. I take the time to give every detail, to explain why I hid Pompon for fear she and Dad would force me to give him away, how I suspected a stranger from the park, then Manie. I explain why Manie took Pompon, and why she lost him by mistake, and how bad everything could have turned out. I tell her how I nearly fell off Manie's balcony and how Pompon could have died alone in the cold. But I didn't give up. I say: Pompon is safely back with his Mummy, and I am, too. Wallace nods. He listens to me and adds a few details to give his point of view.

Mums listens to every word without interrupting.

Then she says: 'I see. Thank you for telling me all this, Tempest, though it's quite late to know. Do you understand the consequences of your lies, the danger you put yourself and others into?'

I nod. Wallace and I both look down. None of us dares to move.

'What did you learn from all this, Tempest?' Mum continues.

I don't answer out loud, but I answer in my head. I learnt that I almost lost my beloved kitten forever for fear of telling the truth. I learnt that the people who I thought were my enemies were actually my friends and meant well: Manie, Steely Blue, Lady Lavender, even Mum. I thought Mum would be crazy furious by now, but she's not. She was scared for me and wants me to understand what I did.

I also learnt that coming forward and asking for help is the best way to solve real problems and that I am stronger if I can count on allies, like I could count on Wallace.

'Mum, I'm sorry I lied to you out of fear. I'm sorry I put myself and others in danger by trying to do everything on my own,' I say, looking straight into my Mum's eyes. I mean it, and I know people look into people's eyes when they mean what they say.

'But I'm also proud I did not give up on my kitten: I looked for him, I followed different trails—some dead ends, some true ones—until I found and saved my cat. And I am proud of that, too.' I add this to show Mum that I am not completely sorry, either. I hold firm onto what I did well. I owe that to myself, too.

'That's true, Tempest; you did very well, given the circumstances, and to recover from your initial mistakes. I give you that,' Mum admits. She's a fair sport.

'Mum?' I attempt, 'I know it's probably not the best time to ask...but Pompon will need a new family in a few weeks, once he's old enough to leave his mummy-cat, Duchess. Wallace and I ... well, we would really, really, **REALLY** love to have him in our family, **PLEASE**, Mummy.'

'Yes, yes! Muuuuummyyyyy pleeaaaaassee,' begs Wallace, jumping on the occasion to join my plea. He's kissing and hugging Mum now, both out of relief and as a seductive Mother-Son strategy that has worked for him so many times before.

'That's too early to decide, guys,' Mum says, 'especially given the lies you told. Having said that, I see how much you care for this kitten. Daddy and I will talk. We want you to be happy more than anything. We will meet Mr Quinn, and we will go see Pompon. If we trust you to be responsible for a pet, and if we can trust you to tell the truth and come for help if you need it instead of trying to get out of trouble all by yourself, then, yes, maybe we can let you have Pompon.' I jump up to hug Mum, feeling all happy inside. She holds me tight against her heart and gives me a big kiss on my tangled hair.

'Yeeeeessssssss! Yeeeeessssssss!' Wallace starts hopping around the kitchen and chants: **'POM-PON! POM-PON! We-will-have-Pom-pon!'**

I know Mum and Dad: it's not a done deal, and we will have to respect the conditions. But I am full of hope.

ONE YEAR LATER

The parents agreed that Tempest and Wallace adopted Pompon. Both children take wonderful care of him, each in their own way. Pompon plays and jumps with Wallace, and he cuddles and explores with Tempest. The kitten has grown into an adult cat, happy and healthy. Pompon knows his way to the park and back and no longer gets stuck in trees. He can visit Eddie and Duchess as often as he likes.

Tempest took Eddie's idea to heart and wrote a book about their adventure. Eddie kept his promise and illustrated it. They sold the book in schools and shops, donating the money to a shelter for lost and injured pets.

Lady Lavender adopted all three of Pompon's sisters so they wouldn't be separated. They love playing among the mint and lavender bushes of her terrace. Tempest, Wallace, and Pompon visit them regularly.

Manie and Lady Lavender eventually became friends. Pompon's sisters still dislike the scent of Manie's Patchouli and her bony fingers, but

Pompon has grown used to it over time.

Life has quieted down, and they might be ready for some new adventures soon…

ACKNOWLEDGEMENTS

My deepest gratitude goes to my husband and children for their unwavering support, love, and encouragement in whatever I decide to pursue.

I am immensely grateful to my family and friends, who so kindly read and commented on the story as it unfolded. Thank you to each and every one of you for your precious support.

The enthusiasm of my young readers touched my heart and gave me the confidence to bring this little story to the world. Thank you to Tristan, Talitha, Judith, Joséphine, Jules, Amy, Alix, Ivy, Uma, Mayah, and to their parents for reading along with the youngest among them.

I am truly grateful to Catherine Watson for her editorial insights, corrections, joyful support, and commitment to seeing this book through to publication.

Special thanks to Nicholas Pelling for his expert veterinary review of Pompon, and to Merril Stevenson for her generosity, attention to detail, and dedication to gathering feedback to make this story better.

Finally, my heartfelt thanks go to Thomasin Chinnery for her kind support and fantastic advice, which led me to the blessing of working with my wonderful illustrator, Macha Yao.

ABOUT THE AUTHOR

Ariane Chapelle is an award-winning author and educator in risk management. While completing a professional textbook, her eight-year-old son asked her to write books for children instead.

Thus, the adventures of Tempest and Wallace were born, inspired by the personalities of her two younger children.

Ariane holds Belgian and British citizenships, and writes in both English and French. She lives in London with her husband and their three children.

Ariane has been dedicated to supporting children and education for many years. All proceeds from this debut novel will be donated to the charity *Children of Klang Leu* (www.enfantsdeklangleu.org), a day-care centre that empowers children's education and provides food, medical care, and social assistance to vulnerable children and their families in Sihanoukville Province, Cambodia.

Printed in Great Britain
by Amazon

52924211R00089